TROUBLE AT THE KENNEL

A Cedar Bay Cozy Mystery - Book 9

BY

DIANNE HARMAN

Published by: Dianne Harman
www.dianneharman.com

Interior, cover design and website by
Vivek Rajan Vivek
www.vivekrajanvivek.com

ISBN: 978-1530074037

CONTENTS

ACKNOWLEDGMENTS

As always, first and foremost, I thank you, my readers for your support. It's hard to believe that this is the ninth book in the Cedar Bay Cozy Mystery Series. In addition to this series I have two other cozy mystery series, Liz Lucas and High Desert, with several books in each. I'm putting the final touches on the first book in a new series, the Midwest Series. I'm more surprised than anyone when I realize all this has taken place in under a year and a half. I've never had so much fun and without my loyal readers, I wouldn't be a successful author!

I'm always asked where I get the ideas for my books. The idea for this book came about when my "granddog" was attacked while he was being boarded at a kennel. That's fact. The rest is fiction. Fortunately, he healed, but the bite was nasty and required extensive surgery.

I would be remiss if I didn't say thank you to the two people who are largely responsible for making my books look good. First there is Vivek, who patiently formats the book for both print and digital, as well as designing wonderfully inventive covers and gives me ongoing marketing advice. And then there is my husband and best friend, Tom. He keeps me out of trouble by mentioning, always very gently, that there's a little issue with a wrong name or a timeline or whatever. Thanks Vivek! Thanks Tom!

Almost forgot to thank my dog, Kelly, (named after Kelly of Kelly's Koffee Shop), for growing up to the point where I can actually trust that when she's quiet she's sleeping rather than getting into trouble. My writing definitely improves when I don't constantly have to get up to check on a dog!!!

Amazing Ebooks & Paperbacks for FREE

Go to www.dianneharman.com/freepaperback.html and get your FREE copies of Dianne's books and Dianne's favorite recipes immediately by signing up for her newsletter.

Once you've signed up for her newsletter you're eligible to win autographed paperbacks. One lucky winner is picked every week. Hurry before the offer ends.

CHAPTER ONE

"Mike, our trip to Cuba was amazing. I'm so glad we went. I still can't believe I've been to Italy and Cuba, and in both places, I got involved solving a murder! I wonder what the chances are of something like that happening. The only down side was that it involved a lot of travel. Kind of a hurry up and wait at all the airports. I can't seem to sleep on an airplane, and last night was no exception.

"I know it's early, but I'd like to go directly to the boarding kennel and pick up the dogs. I really missed Rebel and Lady," Kelly said, as they began the drive from the Portland airport to their home in Cedar Bay located on the central coast of Oregon.

"I missed them too," the burly greying county sheriff said. "We'll go there first, but you better be ready to get out your checkbook. That place is really pricey. The first time I ever saw it was when we took the dogs there on the way to the airport. Any place that has a video camera so you can watch your dog on your iPhone and has a lake behind the barn that was created just for the dogs has got to be expensive. Don't think very many people have it as good as the dogs that stay there do.

"Anyway, back to our trip. When I booked the trip to Italy, I was thinking more of food, wine, cooking, and seeing the sights of Tuscany rather than spending most of my time in an Italian police

1

station helping the chief of police solve a murder. Of course, the *Signor* who owned the cooking school, did tell us when we left that we were always welcome to come back, and he wouldn't charge us because he was so grateful to us for having helped catch the person who murdered his wife."

"I'd happily go back there, plus we did get to spend some time in Florence, and I loved that part of the trip. As far as I'm concerned Mike, it really was kind of like the honeymoon we never got to take right after we were married."

"I agree and you have to admit that Cuba was amazing. The setting was kind of like something you'd read about but never expected to see. Even though I got caught up in helping to solve the murder, I did love the fly fishing. That was pretty spectacular."

"Mike, the one thing I regret is that we couldn't bring Cayo, the stray cat that kind of adopted me, back with us. After all, he's probably responsible for saving my life. I got pretty attached to that little guy. I know it's probably for the best, but..."

She was interrupted by Mike who said in a no-nonsense tone of voice, "That was simply out of the question. Two dogs are enough. We are not starting a zoo and that's final."

"All right. I know that tone of voice."

As they drove down the highway towards Cedar Bay, they spent time reminiscing about recent events and how good it would be to get home. "I know you're not going to like this, but if I could have, I also would have brought Caesar home with me from Italy. I think he would have thoroughly enjoyed living with all of us, but I know that big dog will have a good home with Dominico and his two boys. Hope his wife likes big dogs."

"Kelly, I'm serious. Two dogs are plenty. Lady's a very well behaved dog, actually her name fits her perfectly, and there is no doubt in my mind that Rebel is an old soul. Nothing upsets that dog, but we've peaked on animals. I can't imagine what we'd do with another one. Don't forget, as Beaver County Sheriff, I have to keep the county safe, and you have to keep making people happy by feeding them the comfort food you serve them at Kelly's Koffee Shop. With all the time our jobs require we just wouldn't have time to care for a third dog or a cat. Nope, two dogs are definitely enough for us."

They were about twenty minutes from the kennel when Mike's cell phone rang. Although drivers in Oregon can't legally talk on a cell phone while operating a vehicle, there's an exemption for law enforcement personnel, and Mike took advantage of it. "This is Sheriff Reynolds."

He listened and then said, "I'll be there in about fifteen minutes."

"Oh, Mike, not business. I thought we were going to the kennel."

"We are, Kelly," Mike said grimly. "That was one of my deputies. He's there right now. Your friend, Mary Barnes, the owner of the kennel, has been murdered. Her daughter's on her way there right now. Kelly, there's something else I need to tell you. Whoever did it opened the gates on the dog kennels and released all of the dogs. Mary had two people who stayed at the kennel at night, and they've been able to round up several of the dogs and fortunately Lady was one of them. She's all right, however, Rebel hasn't been found, so keep your eyes peeled. Maybe we'll see him on the way there."

"Oh, no, no! Not Rebel. He knows not to go in the street, but he doesn't know this area at all, and he's probably confused. Mike, we have to find him."

"Kelly, I have to investigate Mary's murder. If we can't find him on the way there, you take the car and start looking for him."

"I just had a horrible thought. The kennel's only about a mile from the freeway. I hope none of the dogs went in that direction."

"So do I, sweetheart, so do I." Even though Mike was driving his own car rather than his official patrol car, he justified his high rate of speed as part of getting to the scene of a crime. In a few short minutes they pulled up to the Doggie Love Kennel and saw the blue and red flashing lights of several sheriffs' cars. Mike and Kelly jumped out of their car and ran up to a deputy who was standing nearby.

"Any sign of Rebel, Ralph?"

"'Fraid not, Mike. Noelle, Mary's daughter, called several people to help look for the dogs, and I called the county animal shelter as well as putting a couple of our deputies on it."

"How many dogs do they think are missing? I know the kennel was the biggest one in the county."

"They estimate around thirty. They were able to find a number of them, and they've been placed in secure kennels. I've cordoned off the murder scene area, but I've been waiting for you. Thought you would want to oversee the investigation."

Mike turned to Kelly and handed her the car keys. "Start looking for Rebel and any other dogs that look like they may be strays or appear to be confused. Keep your phone next to you. If he's brought in, I'll call you."

Kelly ran back to their car, unsure where she should start looking. Her main concern was the freeway, so she began driving the roads that led to it. She drove back and forth on various different roads, trying to set up a grid type of search pattern. The thought crossed her mind that some of the dogs might have just taken off and were running through the nearby brush or residential yards and might make it to the freeway. She resigned herself to the fact that she couldn't do anything about it.

Fifteen minutes later she saw a beagle running alongside the road. She pulled in front of him, got out of the car, and began saying, "Kennel, boy, kennel." The beagle stopped and looked at her. She chided herself for not thinking to bring any dog treats, something she always had in her minivan. She opened the back door of the car and said, "Kennel, boy, kennel." The beagle jumped in the car, and she quickly closed the door behind him. She said a silent prayer of thanks to whoever had taught the beagle the "kennel" command, the one she always used for Lady and Rebel.

A half hour later she'd found three other dogs, but no Rebel. She drove back to the kennel, went through the gate, and yelled to Ralph, "Here are four of the missing dogs. Have someone kennel them. Tell Mike I haven't found Rebel yet. I'm going back out." She put the car in reverse and left the kennel, slowly driving up and down nearby streets. When she neared a school, she slowed down and thought she saw some movement in the bushes next to the school. She stopped the car and looked out the window. There, lying down under a bush, she could just make out the fawn colored coat of a dog who was panting heavily. She opened the back door and began to slowly walk towards the dog, her heart thudding. "Rebel, Rebel, come," she said, hoping against hope it was Rebel. Suddenly the big dog came running out of the bushes towards Kelly, almost knocking her down.

"Easy, Rebel easy. Let's go for a ride. Kennel, boy, kennel. We'll get Lady and go home. No matter what the facts of the murder are, Mike is going to be one happy man when he sees you."

A few minutes later Kelly drove through the gate of the Doggie Love Kennel, and Mike strode towards the car with a big grin on his face when he saw Rebel sitting in the back seat. He opened the door and gave the big dog a hug. "Rebel, I've never been so glad to see a dog in my life. Come on. You look like you could use some water." He walked Rebel over to the big tub of water Mary always kept filled for the dogs.

He turned to Kelly. "Why don't you take Lady and Rebel and go home? I'll get a ride with Ralph when we finish here. There are still about twenty dogs missing. Mary's daughter just got here, and I need to spend some time with her and see if she has any thoughts on why this happened."

"Okay, see you at home." Kelly put Rebel back in the car and walked into the kennel area, found Lady, and took her out to the car.

On the drive home Kelly thought about why anyone would want to kill Mary Barnes, one of the sweetest, most loving women she'd ever met.

And to deliberately release dogs from a kennel? All of them would be unfamiliar with the surrounding area. What kind of a sick person does something like that? Talk about cruelty to animals. I know I've promised Mike several times I'd never get involved in another one of his cases, especially a murder investigation, but this one's personal. If it hadn't been for me, Rebel would probably be a statistic – just one more dog that was killed on a freeway. Thank heavens I found him.

CHAPTER TWO

Susan Yates stood at her window and listened to the constant yelping and barking coming from the Doggie Love Kennel next door. Even though the kennel was situated on three acres of land, she could still hear the dogs, and she hated it.

Darned dogs have it better than I do, she thought. *I can barely make ends meet as it is with the small amount of money I get from the state for being disabled. Lucky my parents died and willed me this piece of property, or I'd be homeless. Be nice if my back didn't hurt so much, and I could clean up the yard, but I'm the only one who lives here, and I don't care. I suppose it really doesn't matter, considering no one ever comes out here anyway.*

She looked out at the rusted washer and dryer sitting next to the driveway and the abandoned car with broken-out windows. Various other items of junk were scattered helter-skelter around the property. Inside the house was more of the same, only worse. She couldn't bring herself to throw anything out, and over the years she'd become a hoarder. Trash and clutter were everywhere. The house was small, almost a dot on the two acres of property that were covered with weeds and dry dirt. There were a few trees here and there. An old rusted chain link fence on three sides of the property separated her from her neighbors. The Doggie Love Kennel had replaced the fencing between its property and hers with a shiny new chain link fence, so none of the dogs could get loose from the kennel through the many holes in Susan's fence.

While she looked out the window, she thought back to how she'd gotten to this place in her life. She remembered when she'd been happily married to Jerry Yates. They'd lived in Cedar Bay in a house that overlooked the water. She'd loved the house with its tubs and baskets that she filled with brightly colored plants. As soon as the plants started to lose their blooms, she replaced them with fresh ones, so there was always plenty of color on the steps leading up to the house and on the patio.

Things started to take a turn for the worse when Jerry lost his job. The sawmill where he'd been employed for many years had closed, and he couldn't find any work. He became despondent and started drinking heavily. One morning she woke up and found a note from him, "Susan, I'm sorry. Goodbye. You deserve better than this. Since most of the lumber that comes into the United States comes from Canada, I've decided to go up there and see if I can find work. I'll call for you when I find a job."

She turned away from the window and sat down, wondering if he was still alive. She'd never heard from him, and shortly after he'd left, she'd fallen over a box someone had inadvertently left in the hallway of the medical building where she'd worked as a receptionist. Het back was injured in the fall. Several operations later her back was no better, and her bank account was depleted. Although she'd been given a personal injury settlement by the insurance company who insured the medical building, it all went to pay for the unsuccessful surgeries. Her parents died in an automobile accident about that time and left their house to her. She couldn't afford to stay in the house she and Jerry had owned, and she let it revert to the bank which had put a lien on it for nonpayment of the mortgage. She'd moved to her parents' home and spent much of her time thinking about the past and how her life was seemingly over.

Mary Barnes, the owner of Doggie Love Kennel had been to see her several times, telling Susan she'd like to buy her property so she could expand her kennel. Susan had nowhere else to go, so each time she'd told Mary no.

She spent many an hour looking out the window towards the barn that had been converted into a kennel with heated and air conditioned rooms for the dogs as well as the artificial lake Mary had a contractor dig, so the dogs could play in the water. Each time she saw Mary and her employees walk out to the kennel to feed the dogs she got angry.

Those dogs have it better than I do. It's not fair. I get hurt and can't work, and my husband loses his job and leaves me, but the dogs get to play in a man-made lake and have plenty of heat and air conditioning. I couldn't even afford to heat this little house last winter, because I didn't have the money. I wonder what would happen if someone released the dogs from their kennels and opened the main kennel gate. Might serve Mary right for being so high and mighty. Maybe she'd never be able to recover from the bad publicity, and she'd have to close the kennel. Then I wouldn't have to listen to the dogs yap all day and night.

She smiled as the beginnings of a plan flitted into her mind, a mind that had become demented over the years from the events that had worn her down to who she was now, a very angry woman.

CHAPTER THREE

Jack Powell sat at his desk deep in thought as he idly let his three dogs lick his hand that was dangling next to his leg. He looked down at Nick, Sheila, and Joe, his beloved pit bulls, and once again became furious. He still couldn't believe Mary Barnes had called to tell him she would no longer let his organization, the Pit Bull Sanctuary, rent a portion of her property at the Doggie Love Kennel. She told him the pit bull rescue dogs that were there would have to be off of her property within twenty-four hours, and it was all because of one little unfortunate incident.

It was still fresh in his memory. Mary had called him and said there had been, as she put it, an incident involving one of the rescue pit bulls. Evidently the manager of the kennel had brought her Labrador retriever to work with her that day. According to Mary the Labrador had intruded in the pit bull's space, and the pit bull had attacked the Lab and almost severed his right rear leg. It required immediate surgery and while the prognosis for the dog's recovery was good, the Labrador's leg was in a splint, and the veterinarian was unsure if the dog would ever again be able to walk normally.

Well, Jack thought, *served the Labrador right for getting too close to the pit bull. Everyone knows dogs need their space, no matter what the breed, and they'll fight to protect it. Fortunately, I was able to find foster homes for the five pit bulls I had on the property I rented from Doggie Love Kennel. Problem is, I don't know where else to go. Mary and her manager have made such a big deal out of it,*

I'm not sure any of the other kennels around these parts will rent space to me. Seems like all the stupid people in the world are always unfairly blaming pit bulls for everything. It's not as if every large dog isn't capable of severing a leg if their space is invaded. Guess the manager threatened to quit immediately because her husband was furious when he found out. It was actually his dog.

Jack thought back to when his love affair with pit bulls had started. He'd been a little boy and his parents decided it would be good for him to have a dog to take care of. They thought it would teach him to be responsible. The three of them had gone to the animal shelter, and from the moment Jack saw the little grey pit bull puppy he later named Lekko, his choice was made. His parents were just as enamored with Lekko. He was a faithful companion to Jack, and his parents never worried about him when Lekko was with him, which was pretty much all the time. Jack and Lekko were so inseparable that his parents became concerned about what would happen to Jack when it was Lekko's time to leave this earth.

One day Jack's father came home from work and said, "Jack, would you help me? I've got something in the car I'd like you to carry in for me." They walked out to the car and there in the back seat was a cardboard box with a beautiful little brindle and white pit bull puppy in it. "Thought Lekko could use a little friend," he remembered his father had said. He'd named the puppy "Tiger," because his markings were about the same as a tiger's. From that day on, Jack had never been without a pet pit bull.

He'd formed the Pit Bull Sanctuary when he became aware of negative comments in the press about the aggressive nature of the breed. When he was young he remembered his mother had always made him cross the street if a Doberman pinscher or a German shepherd was being walked by its owner on the sidewalk. She'd told him they were mean breeds and to steer clear of them. It was only in the last ten years that the focus had switched from those breeds to his beloved pit bull breed, and he felt they were getting an unfair rap.

He began to hear that some kennels wouldn't accept them and animal shelters were filled with the breed. Evidently many people abandoned their pit bulls when the media claimed they were dangerous. He'd met Mary Barnes several years earlier at a dog show. They happened to be sitting side by side watching a beautiful pit bull being shown in the terrier group by its trainer. "Great looking dog," Jack had said.

"Yes, he's a beauty. I'd put my money on him. I'd really like to see a pit bull win. They get so much negative publicity."

One thing had led to another and after Mary and Jack had coffee following the event, he'd told her about his desire to help the breed by starting an organization he intended to call the "Pit Bull Sanctuary." He told her the one thing stopping him was finding a place where he could keep the rescue dogs. Mary mentioned she owned a kennel and had often thought of doing something for the breed. She'd agreed to rent him a piece of her property if he would pay for the fencing required. Mary hadn't wanted to offend any of her long-time customers, many of whom brought their dogs to her kennel for daily playtime, by having pit bulls that were rescue dogs mixed in with the paying customer's dogs.

For several years the arrangement had worked well. Even though Jack was an engineer in his daytime job, his night job consisted of finding homes for the rescued pit bulls. He was usually at the Doggie Love Kennel two or three times a week transporting dogs and generally caring for them. Although his volunteers usually fed and watered the dogs on a daily basis, occasionally he had to fill in for one of them when they were unable to go to Doggie Love Kennel.

He sighed and stood up. He had no idea what he was going to do now that he had no place to temporarily keep the dogs. The incident between the Labrador retriever and one of the rescue pit bulls had happened only a few days ago, and he'd removed all the dogs as soon as Mary had called. The more he thought about it, the madder he got. It wasn't the pit bull's fault. It was the fault of the Labrador retriever for getting too close and the fault of whoever had left the gate ajar. And who was going to suffer? The poor rescue pit bulls.

Serve Mary right if something bad happened at her kennel. Let her know what it feels like to have some major problems. Maybe if all of her dogs were to get loose from Doggie Love Kennel, one of them would attack another dog or even bite a human. Wouldn't be too sorry to see that kennel go under. She wouldn't even give me a second chance.

Take your pit bulls and get out of here. Nice way to do business, Mary. Bet that Lab is still allowed there. Probably asked for it. Yeah, she needs to feel like I do. Think I know just how to go about making that happen.

Jack sat back down and called to his dogs, "Here Nick, here Joe, here Sheila. Here's a treat for my good dogs," he said taking three dog cookies from his pocket and giving one to each of them, while a smile slowly appeared on his face as he came to a decision.

CHAPTER FOUR

When Lisa Collins got into her Jaguar to return home after an appointment with the veterinarian, she made sure her Yorkshire terrier, Duchess, was firmly secured in her dog harness in the back seat. She still couldn't believe what had happened to her precious little dog. The vet had confirmed that Duchess was pregnant, something Lisa had suspected for the last week. The problem was she didn't know who the dog was that was responsible for getting Duchess pregnant. She knew when Duchess was supposed to come into heat and even had a stud lined up, one whose lineage was every bit as good as Duchess's. She became suspicious Duchess was pregnant when she didn't come into heat.

She got home and carried Duchess into her large early 20th century home. Lisa's aunt had raised Yorkshire terriers, and Lisa had become fascinated with the breed when she was a teenager. She'd helped her aunt show her dogs throughout the western states. All Lisa wanted in life was to own the top champion Yorkshire terrier in the United States, as well as Great Britain if it worked out that way. Lisa was fortunate to have been the sole beneficiary of her aunt's sizable estate, most of which could be traced to investments in the lumber industry. Her aunt was a very astute business woman and had sold the family timber holdings and sawmills before the industry fell on hard times.

Her aunt's death occurred while Lisa was in college. She married a fellow student after they graduated, but the marriage didn't last long. Larry Collins was simply no match for the Yorkshire terriers and Lisa's compelling desire to own the top champion in the terrier category. When the marriage ended, Lisa had bought two more Yorkies, hoping one of them would bring her the coveted prize. While they both became champions, it was clear to Lisa neither one would provide her with what had become an obsession, being the owner of the American Kennel Club's dog with the most Grand Champion points for terriers.

Every waking hour found Lisa reading about the dog world, working with her dogs, and developing relationships with breeders. After several years she located a breeder on the East Coast who had a dam who had been the Best of Show at Westminster which had been bred to the Best of Show in Canada. The veterinarian was projecting a litter of five pups. Lisa had sent the breeder a check for $10,000 as a down payment for a female pup from the litter.

When she got the call that the dam had given birth, she got on the first plane she could and travelled to Connecticut to see her new puppy. She paid the breeder the balance of the purchase price and told him she would be back in eight weeks to take the puppy she had named Duchess home with her. Every hope that Lisa had ever had for having the top champion Yorkie was wrapped up in the little ball of fur. No expense was spared for the puppy. The little dog dined on filet mignon and slept in a dog bed with custom-made satin sheets which were changed daily by Lisa's housekeeper.

Duchess was always perfectly groomed. In fact, the groomer came to the house daily to comb out the terrier's silky hair and put a different bow in her hair. On show days the groomer traveled with Lisa and spent three hours getting Duchess ready for her trip around the show ring. Lisa looked at her with adoring eyes as Duchess walked over to her favorite silk cushion and reclined on it.

I have people waiting to buy her puppies. She's everything I ever wanted in a dog. She's not only one of the best Yorkies in the United States, she's also number one in AKC Grand Championship Points, and I'm the one who trained her and showed her. She's only had one litter, but people were standing in line to *buy the puppies, even at the price I was charging, $10,000 per puppy. People told me that was a ridiculous amount of money to ask for a dog, but I just said, "Look at this dog. She's what every Yorkshire terrier should look like," and every one of the litter was sold at full price.*

Lisa walked over to Duchess and gently stroked her soft, silky coat. Duchess looked up at her with her large green eyes, and Lisa could swear she was smiling. Those eyes captivated people when they saw Duchess for the first time. They were emerald green and mesmerizing.

Sweet girl, I am so sorry. I wish you could tell me who the father is. I don't know what to do. The vet said he could perform an abortion on you, but since I'm morally opposed to them, I certainly couldn't do that to you. The problem is, if word gets out you've had a litter and they're a mixed breed, which I'm pretty sure they will be, it might ruin your chances for anyone wanting a puppy from you in the future. Plus, I probably wouldn't be able to get the price for your puppies that I got from the last litter.

Lisa stood up and walked into her office. The vet told her Duchess was about four weeks along. He'd said, which she already knew, that the gestation period for dogs was sixty-three days. When she told him she didn't know how or when Duchess had gotten pregnant, he suggested she look at a calendar and figure out where Duchess might have been twenty-eight to thirty days ago.

She sat down at her computer and pulled up her calendar, trying to re-create where she and Duchess had been four weeks ago. When she looked at her calendar she remembered she'd gone to her nephew's wedding in Las Vegas for three days. It was both his wife-to-be and his second marriage, and they'd decided it would be better to get married in Las Vegas rather than have a big church wedding. Lisa had scheduled an expensive dog sitter to come to the house to be with Duchess while she was in Las Vegas, but the dog sitter had become ill at the last minute, and Lisa had no choice but to put Duchess in a kennel. She briefly considered not going to the wedding, but she knew her sister would never forgive her for putting Duchess above her nephew. She called several people she trusted in the dog world, and Doggie Love Kennel came highly recommended.

Lisa boarded Duchess at the Doggie Love Kennel for three days. That was the only time she'd been away from Duchess during the time frame in question. Duchess must have come into heat a little early, and one of the dogs at the kennel was responsible for the pregnancy.

This really infuriates me. Not only is Duchess pregnant, but I had to pay a special rate for an isolated kennel because she isn't spayed. I was told that any female dog over four months old is required to stay in her own kennel and is not allowed to commingle with the other dogs, because she might come into heat. I had no problem with that, but obviously, something went wrong.

She picked up the phone and dialed the kennel's number. "Doggie Love, may I help you?" a woman's voice on the other end of the phone asked.

"Yes. I'd like to speak with the owner, Mary Barnes."

"Please hold while I get her."

A few moments later a woman's voice came on the line. "This is Mary Barnes, may I help you?"

"Yes, this is Lisa Collins. I believe we've met before. I'm the owner of a Yorkshire terrier, Duchess, that I boarded with your kennel a month ago. There's a little problem that's developed. No, actually it's a very big problem. Duchess is a not only a champion Yorkshire terrier, she is also number one in AKC Grand Champion Points. I have a waiting list of people who want her puppies. The problem is she's pregnant. The vet's certain she's about four weeks along. I didn't breed her. The only place she was during that time frame was in your kennel. I'm certain that one of the dogs there must be responsible for her pregnancy. Believe me, I am not happy about this situation."

"Ms. Collins, I don't like being accused of allowing a situation like that to happen in my kennel. We are very careful here at Doggie Love Kennel. I assure you Duchess was not impregnated during her stay with us."

"Well, Ms. Barnes, I am just as certain it happened when she was there. I'd like to know what you intend to do about it."

"Nothing, absolutely nothing. As I said, we don't allow situations like that to occur here at Doggie Love. Duchess must have been impregnated by one of your neighbor's dogs or something like that. No, I'm certain it did not happen here at Doggie Love."

"Fine. My attorney will be in touch with you," Lisa said, slamming the phone down. *Great, this is just great. I don't know who the father is, the kennel denies any responsibility, and I haven't even addressed whether or not Duchess could be injured giving birth if it turns out the father was some big pit bull or some large dog like that. Sometimes life is so unfair.*

She walked back to where Duchess was sleeping on her satin pillow. "Mama will take care of you, darling. That woman at the kennel deserves to have something bad happen to her for what she's done to my precious baby girl," she cooed. "It's going to be fine. Trust me, I'll take care of it."

Serve Ms. Barnes right if all of her dogs were released from their kennels and allowed to run loose in the neighboring area. Then when a lot more of them get pregnant, she'd probably lose her business from all the lawsuits that would be filed against her, Lisa thought, smiling to herself with a look of satisfaction on her face.

CHAPTER FIVE

After leaving Mike at the kennel so he could continue his investigation, Kelly, along with the two dogs, started driving home. As she drove she wiped away the tears sliding down her cheeks and wondered why someone would want to kill Mary Barnes. She considered Mary to be one of her best friends and found it hard to believe that someone as well-liked as Mary had been murdered.

Putting Mary and the word murder in the same sentence was hard for her to do. She also wondered what would happen to the kennel and the dogs that were boarded there now that Mary was dead. Selfishly, Kelly felt lucky she and Mike had returned when they did. If they'd arrived a day later, Rebel might never have been found. The very thought of losing him caused her to start crying again.

When she approached the driveway of her house she smiled in spite of her tears. She loved the large house that was situated on a hill overlooking the bay. Brightly colored flowers greeted her and the picturesque view of the bay warmed her heart. When the bay was flat and free from waves, the sun shining on it made it look as if diamonds were dancing on the water. It was a sight that never failed to thrill her.

"Come on, guys," Kelly said, "let's go inside." She caught a glimpse of herself in the hall mirror and saw a tall dark-haired middle-aged woman. She thought that maybe Mike's comments about her being attractive weren't said by him just to make her feel good. Lively eyes looked out from a porcelain complexion. She wore her hair pulled up in a chignon, a tortoiseshell hair clip holding it in place. Kelly took a long look at herself, trying to see if she'd gained any noticeable weight while they'd been in Italy and Cuba.

Although she was tall, she wasn't slender and was well aware that eating like she had while she was in both countries could have easily added a few unwanted pounds to a body that obviously liked to eat. She breathed a sigh of relief as she looked in the mirror, glad that if some damage had been done, it wasn't too obvious. She decided she'd eat only healthy food for the next few days to counterbalance the overindulging she'd taken part in while she'd enjoyed the Italian and Cuban food.

The dogs romped from room to room, clearly glad to be home, and ended up in front of the glass patio door, wanting to go out so they could get reacquainted with their own yard. Kelly opened the sliding glass patio door and let them run around in the yard while she brought in the luggage. She spent the next couple of hours unpacking, reading the mail, and deciding what she and Mike could have for dinner, although she knew when a crime had been committed, particularly murder, Mike would probably not make it home until quite late. She was tired from the long trip and had no desire to go to the store.

Mike liked to make a wonderful dish he called "fisherman's fried rice." She decided tonight was the perfect night for the dish Mike had learned to make years ago from his friend, Jack Trout, who had been Mike's fishing guide while they were in Cuba. It only required rice, bacon, eggs, scallions, and a little soy sauce. She had all of the ingredients, and if Mike couldn't make it home, she could easily prepare it herself. After all of the wonderful food they'd eaten lately, she looked forward to a simpler meal. *I'll start my new healthy regime tomorrow*, she thought.

She'd just picked up her cell phone to call Mike and see what he'd been able to find out about Mary's murder when her cell phone rang. She didn't recognize the number on the screen. "This is Kelly

Reynolds."

"Kelly, this is Noelle Hughes, Mary Barnes' daughter."

"Oh, Noelle, I'm so sorry about your mother. I considered her to be one of my best friends, and I simply can't understand how something like this could happen or who would want to kill Mary. It makes no sense. I don't think Mary had an enemy in the world, and everyone I knew loved the kennel. It was definitely the best in the area. I'd just picked up the phone to call Mike and see what was happening when you called. Were you able to find the missing dogs?"

"We've accounted for almost all of them. We're missing two, but considering what we started with, that's pretty good. People are still out looking for them, and I was able to get the local television station to run a story about it. I'm hoping that will help."

"That's certainly good news. I was a nervous wreck when I was driving around trying to find Rebel. I wasn't sure what I'd find, or if I'd even find him at all. Letting the dogs out was one of the most warped things I've ever heard of someone doing. I wonder if the killer did it before or after the murder."

"They don't know at this point. They thought the coroner's report might shed some light on it, but it looks like my mom's murder and letting the dogs out were pretty much done one right after the other. No one knows which came first."

"So if your mother was murdered first, and then the dogs were let out it's quite different from them being let out first and then your mother being murdered. If it's the latter, it could possibly mean she was killed because she saw who let them out. Actually, that makes more sense to me than thinking that someone hated Mary enough to murder her."

"I think so too, but mom seemed to be really rattled during my last conversation with her. It seems she'd had several things happen lately which frustrated her."

"Like what?" Kelly asked.

"Well, evidently a pit bull got out and attacked Sandy Reston's Labrador retriever that she'd brought to Doggie Love for the day. She's the manager of the kennel. Mom said the pit bull almost severed the Lab's leg. It required the immediate attention of a vet and surgery, plus there is no guarantee that the dog's leg will be all right in the future. Mom was so angry, and so was Sandy, that she terminated the lease the Pit Bull Sanctuary had with the kennel. She told the head of it to get his dogs out by the next day. Evidently he did."

"That must have been really hard for her to do, because I know she had a soft spot in her heart for pit bulls. She told me once that she thought they'd been treated unfairly by the press."

"Yes, it was a very difficult decision for her to make. The second thing that happened was a client called her and accused her or one of her employees of leaving her pet's kennel door open and allowing her dog to become impregnated by another dog at the kennel."

"Well, I assume that's not the first time something like that has happened at a kennel," Kelly said.

"Probably not, but this was a little different. The dog who was impregnated is a champion Yorkshire terrier. She also has the most Grand Champion Points in her category. My mother told her it could not have happened at the kennel. The woman was furious and told Mom that her attorney would be calling her. Privately, Mom was a little worried that one of her employees accidently left the dog's kennel door unlocked and a male dog got out, sensed the Yorkie was in heat, and impregnated her. She was worried she might be held financially responsible."

"Oh, that's awful. I feel for the woman, but things like that do happen at kennels."

"Yes, but Mom had a policy that any female dog over the age of four months who wasn't spayed had to be kept in a private kennel which costs quite a bit more. Female dogs that have not been spayed aren't allowed to mingle with the other dogs."

"Well, I suppose both of those people could be suspects, but it seems pretty far-fetched to me. Anything else?"

"Yes. The third thing is that mom had been trying to buy the land just east of the kennel. The woman who owns it has two acres and mom said it was an eyesore, you know, one of those places that has old rusted appliances sitting around in the front yard, lots of weeds, and is generally really unkempt. Mom wanted to buy the land for two reasons. She wanted to expand the kennel, and she wanted to get rid of what she considered to be an eyesore."

"What happened?"

"Mom said the woman who owned it complained a lot about the dogs barking and refused to sell it to her. She told mom if she couldn't stop the dogs from yapping all the time, she was going to go to the county and file a complaint. The woman was so angry about it she said there was no way she'd ever agree to sell her the property."

"Your poor mother. Her last days certainly don't seem to have been very pleasant for her."

"I know. Believe it or not, none of those things are the reason I called you. If you don't mind, I'd like to stop by in an hour or so if you're going to be home. I need to talk to you about something else, and I'd prefer to do it in person rather than on the phone."

"Of course. I'll be here. You certainly have piqued my curiosity. Do you need my address?"

"No, I remember it from the last time I was there. Thanks, Kelly. See you in an hour."

CHAPTER SIX

I hate this job more than 'bout anything else, Ricky Anderson thought as he cleaned out one of the kennels at the Doggie Love Kennel. *The only thing that might come close to takin' my ol' first place hate would be the owner of Doggie Love, Mrs. Barnes. I call her Old Snooty because of her stuck up attitude. She's purty high on my hate list and just might make it to the top real soon.*

Only reason I'm stayin' in this stupid job is 'cause Dad said if I could hold a job for a year he'd give me five thousand dollars. Said workin' here was kind of like goin' into the army. Be good fer me and teach me to be a man. Right. Gave me a choice, and I took this job over goin' into the army. Don't think I'd do too good there. Don't like havin' to take orders from nobody. Anyway, when I get that money, I can get outta town and mosey right on down to Mexico. Seen pictures of bottles of cold beer in metal buckets and lotsa hot wimmen hangin' round everywhere. Sounds good to me. Livin' with Dad ain't no fun. Said he could probably get me a job here. Told me he and Mrs. Barnes go way back, like they had somethin' going' on back in the day when they was young. Right. Can't see either one of 'em havin' anythin' goin' on anywhere or with anybody."

He picked up the bucket of mop water laced with disinfectant, put it in front of an empty kennel, dipped the mop in it, and swabbed out the kennel. He laughed to himself when he remembered how that big pit bull had gotten loose from the fenced-in rescue area and entered the kennel where that little Frenchy lookin' dog was with her silky hair all combed just so perfect and her little pink bow on the top of her head.

She got religion purty quick. Can't blame that big boy fer doin' what comes natcherlly, and boy howdy, did he ever put it to her. That was somethin' to see. When it was over I put him back in the pit bull area. No one was around so didn't have no eyes watchin'. Nobody saw me. It was jes' a guess on Old Snooty's part when she called me in and asked me if I knew anything about one of the dogs gettin' into that pipsqueak dog's kennel and doin' the nasty. Everybody looks down on me. That's another reason I gotta get outta here. Why didn't she ask any of the other people who work here? Jes' me. Tol' her nah. Didn't happen. She asked if I'd made sure all the kennel doors were secured and the gate to the pit bull area was locked. Tol' her sure. First and last things I check every day. Didn't tell her 'bout them open doors. Don' think Old Snooty woulda understood.

He rinsed out the mop and started on the next kennel. Old Snooty had told him they were expecting to be full over the weekend, so she wanted him to clean all of the kennels. She'd told him to work with Anita, the young woman who was in charge of taking the dogs for walks. She said the easiest way to insure that all of the kennels were spotless was for him to stay with Anita, and each time she took a dog for its daily walk, he was to clean that particular kennel. That was in addition to making sure that all of the dogs had water and removing any scum that might be on the lake. She'd also said that the manager of Doggie Love Kennel, Sandy Reston, would be giving him some more things to do as needed.

There was absolutely nothing Ricky liked about his job. If there was anywhere else he could work in Cedar Bay, he definitely would have preferred that job to the one he had, but it was a small town and there weren't many jobs available. It probably hadn't helped that he'd been expelled from the Cedar Bay High School almost a year ago when his history teacher thought he looked like he was high on something when he'd come to class. It was unfortunate that the principal had searched his locker and found a block of marijuana in it. The principal figured out he was the one who had been selling it to some of the students. He also developed a little habit of his own. The principal hadn't wasted any time calling his father and expelling him. Ricky tried to tell them it was an unfortunate misunderstanding, but nobody had believed him. He was gone from good old Cedar Bay High the next day.

His father had been furious when he'd been expelled and had told Ricky that he better get a job or he was going to kick him out of the house. Ricky had applied to the few places in town that had Help Wanted signs in their windows, but Cedar Bay was a small town, and everyone knew that Ricky Anderson had been expelled from high school. None of the business people wanted to take a chance on a kid with a history of selling drugs. The only thing that had come his way was the job at Doggie Love Kennel, and that was only because of his father.

Just a few more months of this, and I'm outta here. Won't ever have to clean a kennel again the rest of my life or take orders from Old Snooty. Won't even have to see my Dad no more. It would be kinda fun to pull Old Snooty's chain, her bein' so high and mighty and all. Might be interestin' to see what would happen if all the dogs got out. That might knock her down a notch or two and serve her right for accusin' me of sumpin, even if I probably was responsible for doin' it. Jes' because the school kicked me out doesn't mean she can accuse me of somethin' without no proof. And there ain't no proof I was the one who didn't double check to make sure a couple of them gates and doors were shut.

Shoot, coulda happened to anyone. I'd give anything to see her chasin' all them dogs and tryin' to get 'em back in their kennels. Man, that would be a sight to see. I could hide and watch, and it'd be kinda like watchin' a reality TV show. Only thing is, couldn't share it with no one, but sure think that's what I'm gonna do. Take that, Old Snooty!

CHAPTER SEVEN

When the doorbell rang an hour later, Kelly looked through the peephole and saw Noelle standing there. She quickly opened the door and hugged the young woman. "Again, Noelle. I am so sorry. I feel like there's a hole in my heart. I've had tears running down my cheeks all day. I can only imagine what you must be going through. Please, come in."

Noelle walked in and was warmly greeted by Lady and Rebel, both of whom maneuvered to get close to her hoping for an ear scratch. Kelly noticed that she didn't seem to be a dog person like her mother had been. "Come on, guys, time for you to go outside." She opened the door and let them out. "Can I get you something to drink, Noelle?" she asked.

"No, thanks," she said as she nervously twisted her hands.

"Noelle, you seem upset by something other than your mother's death. Is that why you wanted to see me? Is there something I can help you with?"

"I hope so, Kelly, I really hope so. See, here's the thing. You know I'm married, actually you were at the wedding." She stopped and took a deep breath. "I don't know what's going to happen to the kennel. My husband Tony, you met him at our wedding, is a cat person, and so am I. We have three cats. Tony and I have no desire to take over the kennel. I don't have any brothers or sisters and dad died several years ago, so I imagine I'll inherit it, but I don't want it. You know Tony and I live in Portland, and we love it there. He's a CPA and really likes the firm he's with. He specializes in tax work involving real estate companies."

"That seems pretty specialized," Kelly said, "and I can understand why you may not want to take over the kennel. I imagine you could sell the land to a developer or maybe someone else would want to buy it and keep it as a kennel. Certainly your mother proved there was a market for a business that caters to dog owners. Plus, hers was a very upscale operation that catered to affluent dog owners that were willing to pay a premium to insure their dog was well cared for. I imagine the kennel was making a nice profit for your mother."

"I just don't know what I'll do. I don't want to make any hasty decisions that I'll regret, and besides, I love my work at the hospital. I'm the head pediatric nurse, and I feel like I often make a difference for the babies. Kind of being their spokesperson, if you know what I mean."

"That's certainly admirable, but I really don't know what any of this has to do with me."

"Did you know my mother used to go to dog shows a lot?"

"No, I don't think she ever mentioned it."

"That's how she met the guy that's the head of The Pit Bull Sanctuary. They were sitting next to each other at a show. Well, Mom became fascinated by the shows, and at the same time fell in love with the German shepherd breed. Anyway," Noelle said as she started to speak more rapidly, "she decided she'd buy a German shepherd puppy from a breeder she'd been watching for years. The breeder's dogs always did well in the shows, usually taking top honors." Noelle leaned onto the edge of her chair and in a nervous rush, blurted out, "I have the puppy in the car, and it needs a home because I can't take it, and I want you to take it." She sagged back in her chair, clearly relieved she'd said what she had come to say.

"Noelle, are you telling me you want me to have your mother's puppy?" Kelly asked incredulously. "When did she get it? She never told me about it."

"She picked it up last week. It's a beautiful little female. She told me she was going to surprise you when you got back from Cuba. Please Kelly, I don't know what else to do with it. I can't take it to the shelter. My mom waited for years for this puppy. Please take her," Noelle said, her eyes bright with unshed tears.

Good grief. This child has been through so much today I don't know how I can say no to her. Mike was very clear earlier today about only having two dogs, but surely we can take her for a couple of weeks until we find a home for her.

"Let's go see this little girl. I assume your mother named her."

"Yes. Her lineage is impeccable. Mom told me her dam was Best of Breed in several shows on both coasts and her sire was Best of Show at the big Madison Square Garden show. The breeder she got her from had a strange requirement that he imposed on anyone who bought one of his puppies. Every dog he sold had to be named for some brand of vodka. How weird is that? Mom told me she stood in front of the vodka display at the liquor store and tried to find one that seemed appropriate. Anyway, mom registered her with the American Kennel Club as Mary's Skyy. I brought everything you'll need for her with me. Mom used the vet in town, Dr. Simpson. I'm sure you know him."

Together they walked out to Noelle's car. The Volkswagen Passat was clearly not a car meant for dogs. "Yes, I know Dr. Simpson quite well. He comes to Kelly's Koffee Shop a lot, and Lady and Rebel consider him a friend."

"Ready, Kelly?" Noelle said as she opened the back door of her car.

Kelly drew in her breath as she stared at the black and tan bundle of fur that looked up at her with soulful looking chocolate brown eyes. She turned to Noelle and said, "She's absolutely beautiful."

Kelly reached down and picked up the puppy who promptly began to lick Kelly's face. "Oh sweet girl, you are absolutely adorable," she said. "No matter how many times I hold a puppy, I'm still a sucker for puppy fur and puppy breath. There is absolutely nothing cuter."

She looked down at the little puppy who continued to shower her with puppy kisses and said, "Okay, I'm sold. I'll take her, but I'm going to have to do some major arm twisting to convince Mike." She continued, "Come on Skyy, time to meet your brother and sister." Kelly turned to Noelle. "This is always the moment I dread, introducing a puppy to an older dog. Well, it has to be done sooner or later. Might as well get it over with."

Noelle followed Kelly into the house carrying the puppy's dog bed and set it down. Kelly opened the sliding glass door for Noelle, and with Skyy in her arms, stepped outside and said, "Rebel, Lady, come meet Skyy. I expect both of you to behave. Before she could even set the puppy down on the grass, Rebel and Lady began sniffing her. Kelly realized she was holding her breath, but she began to slowly exhale when Rebel laid down on one side of Skyy and Lady on the other. In a few minutes all three were asleep.

"Noelle, I'll take the puppy for now, but Mike mentioned today that two dogs were enough. He may not be very happy about this, and in the future I may have to find another home for her. I just want to be upfront with you."

"I understand, Kelly. There's a lot I'm going to have to do in the next few weeks and having one less thing to worry about is a huge relief to me. Thank you so much."

"Noelle, I can never take the place of your mother, but please, if you want to talk or need anything, I'm only a phone call away. You know, I've helped Mike with a few of his investigations, and this one is personal to me. I'd like to see if I can find anything out about who killed your mother. I hope I have your permission to do that."

"Of course, Kelly. If you think something is important, I'm sure it is. This is an area I know nothing about. I'll have to rely on Mike and the homicide detectives from the sheriff's department. I just hope they find out who did it, and he or she is arrested. I know it's still too fresh for me, and I'm probably in shock, but something seems very strange about the whole thing."

"I couldn't agree more. I'll talk to you in a couple of days. If you're going back to the kennel and Mike's still there, I'd appreciate it if you wouldn't say anything about Skyy. It's probably better if he heard it from me."

"I promise. Again, Kelly, thanks."

CHAPTER EIGHT

Kelly fed all three dogs with Lady and Rebel getting their regular dried kibble dog food and Skyy getting a special puppy food Noelle had brought. She spent a couple of minutes looking at the American Kennel Club papers Noelle had given her. They confirmed what Mary had said, the dog had an exceptional lineage. Now it was just a matter of getting the puppy acclimated to her surroundings and getting the other two dogs to accept the new puppy.

At six that evening Mike called. "Mike, I'm so glad to hear from you," Kelly said. "What's happening? Have you found out anything?"

"Not really. I'll tell you about it when I get home. I've got about another hour of work to do here at the kennel. Volunteers found the last two dogs, so all of them have been accounted for. Mary's death was on the early news and several people have already come to the kennel to get their dogs. One even said she didn't want her dog to stay in a place where a murder had been committed. I don't know what the future of the kennel is, but a business person never wants a murder to occur on their premises. Why don't you go ahead and eat without me? I'll fix something for myself when I get home."

"No, I'll wait for you. I'm just putting things in order after being gone so long and figuring out what I need to get done in the next few days." She didn't mention that taking Skyy to the coffee shop and putting her in the pantry storage room for a few days until she got used to the coffee shop was a pretty high priority for her. "Bye love, I'll see you soon."

An hour later, Kelly heard Mike's car pull into the garage. She looked over her shoulder to make sure Skyy looked as cute as she possibly could. She took a chilled glass of wine out of the refrigerator for Mike, hoping it might soften him up a little before he saw the latest addition to the family.

"Hi, sweetheart, figured you could use this after the day you've had," she said, walking into the garage and handing him the glass of wine when he got out of his car.

Mike took it and looked at her appraisingly. "Kelly, I hope you never develop a penchant for poker. You'd lose every time. First of all, the guilty look on your face gives you away, and secondly, you've never brought a glass of wine to me as I'm getting out of my car. You haven't had much time to get in trouble, so what's going on?"

"Well Mike, it's kind of like this. Can you suspend all judgment for a couple of minutes and just enjoy the moment?"

"I could if I knew what was going on. Want to tell me?"

"Umm, I don't think so. Why don't you stand here for a moment with your eyes closed, and I'll put your wine glass on the work bench. OK?"

"Sure, if that's how you want to play this. What are you doing?"

"Just stand there, and I'll be right back in just a minute" She returned with her back to him and said, "Close your eyes and put out your hands."

"Kelly, I've had a very long day, and I'm not particularly in the mood for games. Okay, my eyes are closed, and my hands are out."

She carefully placed the soft ball of fur in his arms and held hers under his so he wouldn't drop Skyy who immediately started licking his face.

"What the devil?" he said opening his eyes and looking down at the puppy. "Where did this come from?"

"This is named Skyy, and she was Mary's puppy. Come on in, and I'll tell you all about it."

Kelly told him about her visit from Noelle and five minutes later he looked at the puppy that was now lying on his shoe and said gruffly, "Kelly, you know I'm not happy about this. I thought we'd decided that two dogs were enough."

"Well, that's not exactly true. You said you thought two dogs were enough. I don't recall me ever saying that, however, I'm sure this is only a temporary thing. We'll just keep Skyy until we can find a new home for her."

Mike reached down and picked up the puppy. "Poor little thing. She must wonder what's going on, first with a new owner last week and now new people this week. That's a lot for a little puppy to take in, although it does seem like Rebel and Lady are pretty good with her."

"They're being excellent. I've always had a theory that housebreaking and training a dog is much easier when there's an older dog to act as a role model. So far Skyy hasn't had an accident in the house and hasn't even tried to chew on something other than the chew sticks and toys Noelle brought with her."

"Well, at least that's good news. Speaking of which I think she should go outside. I get nervous when a puppy starts moving around." He took Skyy out to the back yard while Kelly finished preparing dinner. Rebel got up and accompanied them. A few minutes later Mike returned. "Mission accomplished. Think Rebel's a good influence on her." Kelly turned towards the sink so Mike wouldn't see the smile that had broken out on her face. *He's already beginning to come around*, she thought.

"Kelly, have you given any thought to what you're going to do with this puppy tomorrow when we both have to go to work?"

"Of course. Remember when Lady was a puppy? I took her into work with me, and I can do the same thing with Skyy. Roxie and the rest of the staff will be happy to have an excuse to get outside for a few moments while they walk her, and I'll bet some of the customers would like to as well. I still have the puppy fence I bought for Lady, and I'll put it in front of the entrance to the pantry storage room. It will be fine."

"You're more confident about your abilities in that area than I am."

"It will all work out, you'll see."

"I know. It's that glass half full thing. Right?"

"Right, Sheriff. Now sit down and let me get some food in you."

"What's for dinner?"

"The one thing you taught me to make. Fisherman's fried rice. Sounded perfect, and we had all the ingredients. It's all ready. Time to eat, and then I'll tell you the rest of what Noelle told me, although you may already know."

CHAPTER NINE

"No matter how many times I eat fishermen's fried rice, it always takes me back to the first time Jack cooked it for me," Mike said.

"You may go back in time, but I think it's been an inward thing. I don't remember hearing about it," Kelly said, picking up the dishes and taking them to the sink.

"Several years ago, after a particularly difficult case and when my divorce was being finalized, I needed a little time away from everything, and I gave Jack Trout a call. I'd met him several times over the years, and we always talked about fishing, something both of us were very interested in, although I'd never been fishing with him before. That was the common bond.

"Anyway, he was between guided fishing trips, and we agreed to go up to the Mt. Shasta area for a few days. We camped out overnight, and the first morning I woke up to the smell of coffee and bacon cooking. He fried some rice in the bacon grease, scrambled some eggs, and then mixed it all together. It tasted great on that cold morning. I'll never forget it. Always makes me think of the outdoors and fresh air. I still love the dish. We should have asked him to make it for us when we were in Cuba, but I don't think he had access to the resort kitchen. Thanks for making it tonight."

"I like it because I almost always have the necessary ingredients on hand, and it's so easy to make. That it tastes so good is just a plus. I've taught Charlie how to make it at the coffee shop, and we serve it there from time to time. A lot of people request it even if it's not on the menu. Since I usually have all of the ingredients, Charlie whips it up for them. It's soul satisfying!"

Mike said, "Make you a deal." I'll take Skyy out to see if she can commune with nature one more time while you do the dishes. Sound fair?"

"Very. Take Rebel and Lady with you. I'm sure that little girl can learn some valuable lessons from them."

"Come here, sweet little girl," Mike said, picking the puppy up and walking over to the door. "Lady, Rebel, outside."

Kelly grinned as she saw Skyy lavishing Mike's face with puppy kisses. She turned back to the dishes. *It's just a matter of time until she worms herself into his heart and calling her sweet little girl isn't a bad start.*

A few minutes later the dog parade returned with Mike grinning broadly. "Well, that was a piece of cake. If she continues to be that good, I may have to rethink my two dog rule after all. She is pretty darn cute. She even came to me when I called her, so I guess Mary must have worked with her, because she responds to her name." He sat down at the kitchen table and said, "I kind of remember you saying something about Noelle telling you about a conversation she'd recently had with her mother, and it might have something to do with her murder."

"I don't know about it having anything to do with her murder, but there were three people who Mary recently had words with." She told him about the Pit Bull Sanctuary man, the Yorkshire terrier pregnancy incident, and the neighbor who was upset about the excessive barking coming from the kennel.

Mike listened carefully and then said, "Well, I suppose all three could be considered as suspects, but I have a hard time making any of them as killers. Yes, they were all probably angry at Mary for various reasons, but angry enough to kill? I think it's a stretch, Kelly."

"I have no idea. I'm simply telling you what Noelle told me. She did mention that Mary was very upset over the incidents."

"That's understandable, but to kill someone and release all the dogs? Of course we still don't know which came first, Mary's death or the dogs being released. What I want to do tomorrow is look at the kennel's business records and talk to the manager, Sandy Reston. She might know something. Actually she probably would know more than Noelle, since she was the one who was working there. What's on your agenda for tomorrow?"

"Business as usual. I'm glad I only have one day before the weekend. It will allow me to ease into the routine. I need to get some groceries for here, and I'm sure I'll have to restock the coffee shop. I'll take Lady and Skyy with me. Rebel's been going into work with you lately, so he'd probably be more comfortable doing that. Okay?"

"That's fine. If I get tied up on this investigation, I'll give you a call. Might even stop by the coffee shop for lunch and see how this little girl's doing," he said looking down at Skyy who was sound asleep and lying on his shoe. "What do you intend to do with her tonight?"

"I have an old wire kennel out in the garage. Thought I'd put her in that. I'll get up in the middle of the night and take her out along with one of the other dogs. Usually dogs are pretty good when they're in their kennel."

"Since you're the one who said yes to Noelle, I'll willingly let you do that. Think we both need to get to bed. Between the travel, the murder, and what I know will be a busy day tomorrow, this man needs some sleep, and I think you could use some too. What an end to a great trip. I think we're snake bit when it comes to having a quiet peaceful vacation from the beginning to end."

"Yeah, I know what you mean, but you're right, I could definitely use some sleep. It's been quite an emotional day between not being able to find Rebel and worried if I did find him there was a good chance it wouldn't be pleasant. That, along with the murder of one of my closest friends and the addition of a new member to our family. Yes, I definitely need some sleep."

"Kelly, it's a temporary addition to our family, not a permanent addition. Remember that," he said over his shoulder as he walked down the hall towards the bedroom.

Uh-huh. With that attitude I probably won't be telling you about the dog show that starts tomorrow afternoon at the fairgrounds. Think I'll pay it a visit, and see if I can find out anything about the pit bull man and/or the Yorkie lady. Anyway, with Skyy's lineage I probably should become familiar with what goes on in the world of dog shows.

CHAPTER TEN

The next morning Kelly had to be at the coffee shop at 6:00 a.m. to get everything ready for the doors to open for the hungry and thirsty customers at 7:00 a.m. She parked in her usual spot next to the pier. Lady jumped out of the minivan when Kelly opened the back door for her, and then Kelly carefully carried the small kennel with Skyy in it to the front door of the coffee shop. She had just unlocked the door when she heard Roxie, her longtime waitress say, "That may be about the cutest puppy I've ever seen. Do the Reynolds have a new addition to the family?"

Kelly put the flat of her hand out and wagged it back and forth in the well-known gesture for "maybe yes, maybe no." She picked up the kennel and walked into the coffee shop followed by Lady and Roxie. In a few minutes they were joined by Madison, who worked as a part-time waitress when she wasn't in class at the cosmetology school she was attending, and Charlie, Kelly's longtime fry cook.

"Let me guess, Kelly," Roxie said. "You're back from vacation, and I know you boarded your dogs at the Doggie Love Kennel while you were gone. The news station had a long segment on the owner's murder and about the dogs being set loose, so my guess is this puppy has something to do with that."

"Very perceptive, Roxie." She told them what had happened and how Mary's daughter had asked her to keep the little puppy, at least for a while.

"Well, perceptive as I am, I'd be willing to bet Mike isn't nuts about the idea of having three dogs. You were kind of stretching it when you got Lady, as I recall."

"Yeah, I'm not sure what's going to happen, but for now I have her. I'm going to put her in the storeroom with the fence up. If any of you have a spare minute, I could use a little help walking her outside. I'm having really good luck if Lady or Rebel goes with her, so you might want to take Lady as well. This little girl really is sweet." Kelly walked back to the storeroom and got Skyy settled while the other three went about their morning duties.

At 7:00 a.m., like it did every morning, the coffee shop began filling up. Everyone wanted to find out the latest gossip about the murder of Mary Barnes and the dogs being released at the kennel. Kelly's Koffee Shop was always the place people came to get the latest gossip and this particular morning was no exception. The room was abuzz with questions, comments, and speculations. Kelly took Skyy out a couple of times, but the third time she went back to the storeroom she noticed the fence was down and Skyy was missing.

She walked over to the cash register where Roxie was ringing up an order and said, "Roxie, do you know what happened to Skyy? I can't find her, and I can see Madison and Charlie, so neither one of them has her."

"Yup. You were talking to a couple of the customers, and I saw Mike go in the back and take her outside. If you look through the window blinds, you can see him holding her and talking to some people a couple of yards down the pier."

"That's interesting. He didn't even bother to say hello to me, but he takes Skyy out and holds her? And he's the one talking about having her only be a temporary addition to the family?"

"Kelly, I'm not a wealthy woman, but I'd bet everything I have that Skyy will be a permanent addition to your family. Mike might like to act like a gruff tough sheriff, but the way's he's holding Skyy is anything but that."

"I think you're right, at least I hope so. I don't think I mentioned that Mary's daughter told me her mother had really done her research before she bought Skyy, and she comes from an incredible lineage. She even told me Mary expected she could easily be Best in Show. I don't know much about dog shows, but I have to admit my curiosity's aroused."

"I don't blame you. Matter of fact, I saw where a big dog show is being held out at the fairgrounds. It starts today and goes through the weekend. You might want to check it out. Are you thinking of showing her?"

"I have no idea. This is all completely new to me, but I have to admit I'm kind of fascinated. I saw an ad in the paper for the show and thought I might go after work this afternoon."

"As many times as Mary was in here and as close as she was to you, it's kind of strange she never said anything to you about her wanting a dog to show."

"I thought the same thing and mentioned that to her daughter, Noelle, and the only thing we could figure out is that her mother probably wanted to keep it quiet so she wouldn't be hounded by people coming to the kennel and talking about it. It's one thing to be Jane Q. Public and think about buying a dog to eventually show, but it's quite another when you're the owner of a well-known kennel. I'm sure she knew a lot of people in the dog breeding world, many of whom would love for her to buy their puppy. It would give them bragging rights. At least that was our supposition."

Just then the door to the coffee shop opened, and Mike walked in with Skyy nestled in his arms. "Hi, sweetheart. Thought I'd pop in and see how your morning's going. When I got here you were busy, and I saw Skyy in the storeroom. I thought I'd save you the trouble of having to take her outside. I'll put her back."

"Mike, Kelly, who is this? A new addition to your dog family?" Doc, a longtime customer and friend of Kelly's and Mike's asked as he strode over to them. Kelly had been instrumental in helping Doc resume his medical practice after he'd been unfairly found liable for damages for the death of a young female patient of his. He'd even been the best man at Kelly and Mike's wedding.

"Well, she's kind of collateral damage after the murder of Mary Barnes at the Doggie Love Kennel, so yeah, we have her for a little while," Mike said.

Doc reached out and petted Skyy who promptly thanked him with enthusiastic puppy kisses. "If I were a betting man, I'd bet on the puppy. Don't see that one leaving the Reynolds home anytime soon," he said winking. "What's her name?"

"Doc, her name is Skyy. She's named for a vodka brand. The breeder had a policy that every dog he sold had to be registered with the American Kennel Club with the name of a vodka brand somewhere in the registered name."

"That's a first, but the name Skyy is cute. By the way, Mike, what's the latest word on the murder and letting all those dogs out? Anything you can say publically?"

Mike ruefully said, "There's nothing I can say privately or publicly. At the moment I have absolutely nothing to go on. I spent the morning looking over Mary Barnes' financial records, and I didn't find anything of interest in them. Matter of fact, the kennel was doing quite nicely. I guess Mary justified the high prices she charged by having the artificial lake, the computer streaming, and the top of the line individual kennels for each dog. This afternoon I'm going to spend some time with the manager. I'm hoping she can tell me something."

"Mike, why don't you sit down and order something. I'll put Skyy back in the storeroom," Kelly said as she took the puppy from Mike and started to walk away. Skyy began whimpering, and Kelly turned back to Mike, "Did you hear that? I think you have a new friend."

"Give her back to me. It's okay, girl. I'm right here." Skyy became perfectly quiet as Mike scratched her ears. Roxie, Doc, and Kelly all looked at Mike and grinned.

"Temporary, you say, Sheriff? Sure," Doc said as he walked over to his favorite stool at the counter and ordered his usual luncheon special.

CHAPTER ELEVEN

At three o'clock that afternoon, the usual closing time for Kelly's Koffee Shop, Kelly locked the door and walked to her minivan with Skyy's kennel in one hand and her leash with Skyy attached to it in the other hand. Lady trotted next to her, but Skyy felt it was her personal calling in life to stop and sniff everything she came across.

Good grief, Kelly thought. *This is taking twice as long as usual. Think I better take them both home before I go out to the dog show. Mike mentioned he'd probably have to work late, so I have a little time.*

Thirty minutes later she parked her minivan in the county fair parking lot. She was amazed at how many people were attending the dog show on a Friday afternoon. Kelly had never been to a dog show before and was really looking forward to it. She paid the entrance fee, stopped at a stand where a free newspaper about the dog show was being given away, and walked into the big hall. Several show rings had been set up and there were grandstands in front of each so people could sit and watch while the dogs were being shown.

Kelly walked over to a group of people that were looking at the dogs in the ring in front of them. "Excuse me," she said to a man who looked like he knew what he was doing. "This is my first dog show. Are there different rings for different breeds?"

"Yes. Go back to the entrance and pick up a schedule that tells what time each breed is going to be shown and on which day. Today's shows are pretty much for puppies and dogs that need to get some points towards their championships. Tomorrow and Sunday are the big days. Saturday is the competition for the Winner's Dog and Winner's Bitch. Sunday is the grand finale. That's when the best dogs compete for Best of Breed. It's a pretty big deal. If a male wins, his stud fee can be increased, and if a female wins the puppies in her litter become pricier."

"So there's quite a bit of money to be made if your dog gets one of the top prizes, is that right?"

"It's kind of a twofold thing. Some people follow the show circuit for the money. They want to have their dog win Best of Breed. It guarantees that stud fees and puppies will earn a lot of money for them, but there's another thing operating here as well. It's called ego. For many people it has nothing to do with money. It's all about them owning the dog that has been declared Best of Breed. For a lot of people, it's the single biggest achievement they'll ever have in their lives. Believe me, you'll see the same people at the next show. Their entertainment is following the shows, showing their dogs, and hoping someday to be a winner."

"So from what you're saying, these dogs are not family pets."

"Absolutely not. If you want to see something really interesting, go back behind the show ring area and take a look at the grooming area. That's where owners and groomers do the last-minute grooming of their dogs just before the dog enters the ring. Do you know what a snood is?"

"Vaguely. Isn't it something that covers women's hair?"

"Yes. It originally came from Europe. Many years ago unmarried women wore snoods. Well, the basset hound owners started putting them on their dog's ears after the groomer finished with them and before the dog went into the ring. It protects the dog's ears from touching the floor and getting dirty."

"Are you kidding? That's unbelievable."

"Trust me," the man said. "That's nothing. All of the owners and handlers keep a dog tack box for each dog. It has hair spray, powder, hair dryers, and whatever else they feel is needed for the dog to look his or her best in the ring."

"Thank you. I had no idea there was so much involved in preparing a dog to be shown. I thought the owners came, the dogs were walked around in a ring, and everyone went home. Sounds like there's a lot more to it than that."

"There is. Being a dog handler is a full-time profession. They usually charge somewhere between $50 and $100 per dog to show them, and often they show a number of different dogs in a day. Many of the handlers have large trailers or recreational vehicles they use to transport the dogs from show to show. A dog may spend months with a handler. Keep in mind that this show is not Westminster, plus there's usually a bonus structure for wins at various levels such as Best of Breed or Best in Show."

"This is amazing. It seems like a completely different world."

"It is. It's not just running around the ring. The handlers have legal contracts with the owners, and they have to work closely with veterinarians to make sure the dog is in optimum health. It's a very big responsibility, and handlers that can get a dog to Best of Breed or Best in Show are in huge demand. They can pretty much name their own price."

"Thanks again. I'm going to go get the schedule. There are a couple of breeds I'm interested in."

"What would those be, if you don't mind me asking?"

"I'm curious about pit bulls," Kelly said. "I have a boxer, and I know that both breeds are considered bully breeds, but I'd like to see what really good pit bulls look like. So often the only time I see them is when they're with some macho man and the dog's wearing a spike collar. I always wonder if it's a purebred."

"You won't see any spike collars here. Everyone takes their dog's breed very seriously. What's the other breed?"

"I find Yorkshire terriers interesting," she said thinking about what Noelle had told her. "I guess if any breed would benefit from grooming it would be them. They certainly have a lot of long silky hair that would have to be attended to."

"Well, you should have an interesting time. I can't think of two breeds that would be more diametrically opposite from one another. Excuse me, but that's my dog that just went into the ring."

"Good luck," Kelly said, "and again, thanks for all the information." She walked to the front desk and picked up the schedule for the weekend.

Good, both of the breeds are going to be shown within the hour. While I wait, I can read the free paper that was being handed out about the dogs and see if I can find out anything about the pit bull man and the Yorkshire terrier woman. I'll have enough time to watch the two breeds when they're shown in the ring and then head home in time to start dinner before Mike gets home.

CHAPTER TWELVE

On her way to the ring where the pit bulls were going to be shown Kelly passed a sign on a door that read "Grooming Area – Authorized Personnel Only." Based on the conversation she'd just about the dogs' groomers, she decided to take a quick look. She opened the door and stood there with her mouth agape. Everywhere she looked there was activity. The noise level was almost deafening from the sound of the hair dryers. All kinds of breeds were standing on small tables with their groomers next to them who were wearing aprons while they were fluffing, dusting, curling, and even applying clear nail polish to dogs' toenails.

She quickly closed the door and stepped back outside the room before anyone discovered she wasn't authorized to be in there.

That's amazing. If anyone had tried to describe that scene to me I would have said they were crazy. I can't begin to imagine how much money must be spent by the dog owners for groomers and supplies. Of course that doesn't take into account the huge cost of buying the dogs in the first place. This is not a cheap pastime. Interesting as it is, I'm so glad I never had any desire to show my dogs. I'm fine with them curling up at my feet at night and giving them an occasional brushing and a bath. Even if Mike decides we can keep Skyy, I'm not sure I'm ready for that world.

She walked to the ring where the pit bulls were just starting to be shown. Although there were a number of dogs in the ring, there weren't many people watching. Kelly sat down and looked at the dogs. Unlike the other breeds being shown where all the dogs looked like one another except for coloring, these dogs were all over the board. No two seemed to look alike.

"Excuse me," Kelly said to the man sitting in front of her. "Why are there so many variations in the way these dogs look?"

"I really don't know that much about the breed. See that man sitting over there wearing a blue shirt? He's very knowledgeable about the breed. Matter of fact he's the head of the Pit Bull Sanctuary. He's the one you ought to talk to."

"Thanks, I'll see if he can help me." She remembered what Noelle had said to her yesterday about the man that ran the Pit Bull Sanctuary and couldn't believe how lucky she was that she might have an opportunity to talk to him.

She walked over to the man wearing the blue shirt, sat down beside him and said, "Hi, I'm Kelly Reynolds. I'm curious about the pit bull breed and the man over there suggested that I talk to you. He said you were really knowledgeable about them."

"Sure, happy to talk about my favorite subject. This breed is a little different from most of the other breeds. As a matter of fact, I own three pit bulls, and they're all as different as night and day. There are four different organizations that set standards for the breed and they vary. There's the United Kennel Club, the American Dog Breeders Association, the All American Dog Registry, and the last one is the American Kennel Club. They all have slightly different standards. AKC uses the standard for the American Staffordshire terrier. Then it gets really interesting because the terrier can also be registered with the UKC as an American Pit Bull Terrier."

"I would think that would be very confusing to people who are buying their first one and would like to show it."

"It is. There are standards, even within each of those clubs, but the problem occurs when a dog is registered with one of them, and the owner decides to breed the dog to increase its size or whatever. Although the dog is not quite up to the particular standard for that group, he still can be registered with one of the other groups. It really makes it difficult for the judges. They have to be very aware of the standard for the particular club that is hosting the show."

"Are new owners told about these differences?" Kelly asked.

"I can't answer for all of them, but I can tell you that the people I bought my three dogs from never gave me that information. I doubt if they even knew about it. I found out the hard way. The first show I ever entered was an AKC show. My dog had the standard for the American Dog Registry, so I got nowhere. I never made that mistake again."

"So you have three pit bulls? No wonder the man over there said you were very knowledgeable about the breed."

"I've had pit bulls all my life, and I still like to come to dog shows to see them. Once mine get enough points to make champion, I stop showing them. As a matter of fact, I took the afternoon off from work today, so I could come to this show. I could easily breed them and get quite a bit of money for their puppies or stud fees, but I think what's happened to their reputation the last few years is horrible. I actually started and presently run the Pit Bull Sanctuary. I try to find homes for dogs whose owners no longer want them."

"I've heard of your group. My husband and I board our dogs at Doggie Love Kennel, and I remember in one of the newsletters the owner mentioned that your group was renting space from her, but separate from the boarded dogs. We just got home from a trip yesterday, and I was at the kennel to pick up our dogs, but I didn't see any pit bulls."

"I'm sure you didn't. Evidently there was a problem about a week ago. It seems like one of the rescue dogs got out of the area where they were kept and attacked the manager's dog causing some severe injuries to the dog. Knowing the breed, I'm sure the pit bull was provoked. Usually they're very gentle. Anyway, the owner of the kennel called me and told me to get all the pit bull rescue dogs off of her premises by the end of the following day. Fortunately, I have a few people I can call on who are always willing to take a rescue dog."

"When we went to pick up our dogs," Kelly said, "we learned that someone had let all of the dogs in the kennel loose a few hours before we got there and the owner of the kennel had been murdered. Fortunately, they were able to find all of the dogs, including both of our dogs. We couldn't believe it. It was so sad."

"Yeah, I heard on the news last night that the owner, Mary Barnes, had been murdered, and the dogs that were boarding there had all been released by someone, probably the killer. Don't know anything about it, but if she treated others the same way she treated me, I'm not surprised someone killed her. Matter of fact, I kind of felt like it was karmic justice. She sure turned her back on the dogs that were in need at the Pit Bull Sanctuary, so if someone decided to do something bad to her, I can't say I'm sorry."

Kelly sat back and turned her attention to the dogs in the ring, thinking about what the man had just said.

He certainly could qualify as a suspect. Sounds like his whole world is dogs and his love for the pit bull breed. Being forced to remove the dogs from the kennel property on almost no notice might have made him mad enough to want to commit murder. Since Mary had a policy of not accepting pit bulls for boarding, he might have felt she was discriminating against him and his beloved breed and needed to be taught a lesson, twisted as it seems. Probably better tell Mike about this guy, and Noelle did say her mother was concerned about him. What a coincidence — that the man I talked to suggested I speak to the head of the Pit Bull Sanctuary who just happened to take time off from work and come to the dog show today. Small world. Seems like a nice enough man, but you never know about people, particularly when they're obsessed with something, and there is no doubt in my mind this guy is obsessed with pit bulls.

"Thanks for taking the time to talk to me."

"You looked so familiar to me when you walked over, and I just remembered that I've seen you at your coffee shop. I've been there for breakfast several times. I'm Jack Powell," he said, extending his hand.

"Yes, I'm the owner of Kelly's Koffee Shop. Again, thanks for taking the time to educate me about pit bulls. I've got to be going because I want to see a couple more shows. I'll look forward to seeing you sometime at the coffee shop."

CHAPTER THIRTEEN

Kelly sat in the grandstand next to the show ring where the Yorkshire terriers were going to be shown. She pulled out her iPhone to access the Internet and see if she could find out what was special about the breed besides their long silky coat. She learned the breed had been very popular in England during the Victorian era, particularly for its ability to catch rats. It now ranked sixth in popularity in the United States.

The site she was looking at went on to say that originally the bluish-grey dogs were mostly owned by members of the working class, particularly weavers. A lot of facetious comments were made about their silky coats being the ultimate product of the weavers' looms. At about ten pounds, it was a breed that was very good for today's modern apartment and condominium living. She smiled to herself thinking about Lady and Rebel who were big dogs, and knew that Skyy was also going to be about their size. Her dogs easily outweighed the Yorkies by seven or eight times.

She had about fifteen minutes before the next round of Yorkies were to be shown, so she picked up the dog show paper she'd been given when she'd paid her entrance fee and glanced through it. A headline caught her attention and she read "Any Truth to The Rumor About Duchess the Yorkie? By The Dog Who Nose." There was a cartoon drawing below the headline of a Yorkie with a dog next to it that resembled a bloodhound with its nose on the ground, sniffing.

Kelly smiled and thought that was a pretty cute way to do the column. She remembered when Noelle had told her about the prize-winning Yorkie who had allegedly gotten pregnant at Doggie Love Kennel, Noelle had mentioned the name "Duchess." She began reading the three paragraph article.

"Yorkie dog breeders are wondering if there's any truth to the rumor that Duchess, the Yorkie terrier with the most Championship points, is pregnant and the owner doesn't know who the father is. The Dog Who Nose contacted the owner who declined to speak about it.

Several knowledgeable Yorkie breeders have suspected that Duchess is pregnant, particularly since she hasn't been entered in the show being held this weekend at the fairgrounds. The Dog Who Nose says that Duchess' owner always shows her at local shows, if for no other reason than to bring her to the attention of people who might want to buy one of her puppies.

The Dog Who Nose is pretty sure the rumors are true. No Duchess at shows and no mention of Duchess' puppies up for sale – a combination that almost insures that Duchess is pregnant, but not by the stud her owner was hoping would be the sire. Stay tuned and when The Dog Who Nose has more information, you'll be the first to know."

Wow, Kelly thought. *This really is a different world. I'll bet the owner isn't too thrilled with this article. And to think that everyone who comes to this show can pick up the newspaper and read about Duchess.*

When she put the paper down she noticed that the dogs were being brought into the ring by their handlers. Each of the dogs that was trotting around the ring had been fluffed, combed, and carefully groomed. She smiled, thinking they looked like they should be sitting on chaise lounges having champagne served to them by attentive maids or butlers. These dogs didn't look like they belonged to the working class, but instead would be more at home with a member of the aristocracy.

While she was sitting there mulling over the grooming of her dogs, which was practically nonexistent, versus the Yorkies' grooming, she overheard a conversation taking place behind her.

"Susie, it's good to see you," a woman sitting behind her said as the woman named Susie sat down next to her. "Kind of interesting that Lisa doesn't have Duchess in the ring. I remember Lisa saying that Duchess was going to be coming into heat. Makes me think that the article by The Dog Who Nose might be right. Have you heard anything? Is that why they're not here?"

Kelly realized they were talking about the woman Mary had been concerned was going to sue the kennel, the one Noelle had mentioned.

"Probably," the woman named Susie answered. "A good friend of mine works for Dr. Simpson, and he confirmed that she's pregnant, but evidently Lisa is furious about it."

"Why would she be furious? From what she gets for the puppies that are in Duchess' litters, I'd think she'd be ecstatic."

"Normally she would be. I guess you didn't read the article very thoroughly because there's a little problem with this pregnancy. I know you're discreet, Gina, but I would appreciate it if what I tell you isn't repeated. You know how people in the dog world like to gossip. The mere scent of a scandal and the rumors start. I really don't want to get involved in something like that, plus I promised my friend I wouldn't say anything."

"I understand. Susie, you know you can trust me. What's going on with Duchess, and no, I just glanced at the article."

"Well, from what my friend overheard Lisa telling Dr. Simpson, it seems like she went to her nephew's wedding about a month ago. The woman she usually uses to dog sit Duchess became ill and had to cancel. She called several people she knows who have champion dogs, and they all said the best kennel for boarding, if you had to do it, was the Doggie Love Kennel. She left Duchess there over a weekend."

"I know the kennel, and it's excellent, but did you know the owner was murdered yesterday? I also heard that someone released all the dogs from their kennels. Can you imagine what would have happened if Duchess had gotten out? One look at her, and I'm sure she'd be stolen and wind up in one of those terrible puppy mills."

"Yes, I heard the same, and when I tell you what happened, you'll understand why my friend heard Lisa tell Dr. Simpson that she thought the owner deserved to be murdered. She said she was so angry she could have killed the owner herself."

"Wow, that's so unlike Lisa. What happened?"

"Well, she left Duchess at the kennel and arranged for her to have a special kennel because the owner has a policy that any female dog that's not spayed and could come into heat has to have its own special kennel, and they cannot be around any of the other dogs. And from what my friend said, those kennels don't come cheap. Lisa said it was almost like she was being punished for not having Duchess spayed."

"I've boarded Fluffy there, and I felt the same way. So what happened?"

"A week or so ago she said she noticed that something seemed to be off with Duchess. She told Dr. Simpson that she waited a few days thinking that her loss of appetite and lack of energy were due to a touch of the flu or something like that, but then Lisa became suspicious and made an appointment with Dr. Simpson so he could examine her. He confirmed she was pregnant. He wanted to know who Lisa had bred her to because he followed the dog shows and knew most of the other Yorkies that were quality show dogs like Duchess."

"Well, so who is the proud father? Like the vet, we know most of the champions in the breed."

"That's the problem, Gina, she didn't breed her to a Yorkie or any other dog for that matter. Dr. Simpson told her Duchess was about four weeks pregnant, and she should check her calendar and try and reconstruct where she might have been at that time. It turns out that was when she'd boarded Duchess at the Doggie Love Kennel.

"She called the doctor after she got home and told him she'd taken Duchess to the Doggie Love Kennel that weekend. She said someone must have left the door of her kennel ajar and some male dog got into Duchess' kennel. Lisa told him what really worried her was she has no idea who the father is. She's afraid it might be some very large dog, and if that's the case, Duchess could very well have problems delivering the puppies. My friend said she was calling the doctor almost every day, and the doctor was getting pretty tired of all the drama."

"Do you know if she called the kennel when she realized Duchess had probably gotten pregnant during the weekend when she was at the kennel?" Gina asked.

"Yes," Susie said, "but she told Dr. Simpson it sure didn't do her any good. She said she'd spoken to the owner, a woman named Mary. She's the one who was murdered yesterday. The owner denied having any knowledge of Duchess' door being left open and actually told Lisa she had to be mistaken. She said it could not have happened at her kennel. She was in a state of total denial. Lisa told the doctor it was not a good phone call. It ended with Lisa telling the owner that her lawyer would be calling her, and you know Lisa. With all her money, she has a lawyer on a permanent retainer."

"Now that the owner of the kennel is dead, do you think she'll go ahead and sue the kennel?"

"I don't think so. My friend told me Lisa said she was just glad the owner was dead, and she hoped the kennel would be bulldozed and the land sold to some developer. She was worried it could not only be the end of Duchess' career, but it could even be the end of her life. And all because somebody left the door to her kennel open."

"That really is a shame. Duchess is one of the best Yorkie terrier show dogs in the country. I think Lisa even told me once she had a waiting list of people who want her puppies, and they are very expensive What about terminating her pregnancy? I know that's an option."

"I wondered the same thing. I guess Lisa is morally opposed to abortions and feeling that way, she couldn't allow her dog to have one. Dr. Simpson said about the best thing she could hope for if she wasn't going to allow an abortion was to hope Duchess had a miscarriage."

"As a dog owner, I can understand how she feels. That is so sad."

"I know. There's a good chance she could be injured giving birth to the puppies and never be able to have another litter. Plus, Lisa might not be able to show her again if she's injured, to say nothing of the fact that she might die delivering the puppies."

"I honestly don't know what I'd do in that situation. The one thing I do know is I'd be furious!"

"From what I hear she was and is. Oh, look. Fluffy's doing really well. The judge just motioned to your handler. Congratulations!"

"Thanks, I better go down to the ring. Fluffy likes to see me as soon as she finishes a show." She stood up and started walking down to the ring. Kelly got up from where she'd been sitting, and walked towards the door. As she was walking out, she happened to be behind the woman who had been talking to Susie. The woman stopped in front of another woman, bent down in front of the other woman and said in a low voice which Kelly could barely hear, "Cindy, you won't believe what happened to Duchess. I'll call you and tell you all about it."

Well, Kelly thought, *so much for not breathing a word of it. I've read where dog shows are viciously competitive, but to promise someone you won't tell anyone about a confidence and then a moment later renege on your promise is really wrong. Guess she wants Fluffy to be the number one Yorkie, and with Duchess out of the running, she very well might be. It sounds to me like Lisa had a motive to commit murder, and she's very angry. That's a combination that easily makes for another suspect. Time to head home and see if Mike's found out anything.*

CHAPTER FOURTEEN

"Hi, everybody, I'm home," Kelly said to the two big dogs who greeted her as soon as she walked into the house from the garage. "Come on guys, let's get Skyy out of her kennel and take her outside. You two could probably use a little time in the yard as well."

A few minutes later Kelly saw all three dogs frolicking around in the back yard, two big ones and one little one who kept herself busy aping whatever the big ones were doing.

Puppies need to eat a lot and even though she's been fed twice today, I'll bet she's hungry. I'll take care of all three of them before I start our dinner. Fortunately, none of them is food possessive, and I can put all of their dog dishes with food in them on the patio.

She carried the three plastic bowls to the patio, pink for Lady, light blue for Skyy, and dark blue for Rebel. Within minutes, the food had been eaten. Kelly refilled the big water dish she kept on the patio for them and let them back in the house.

Mike's probably had a long, tough day, and there's nothing better than a good meal at the end of one of those kind of days, Kelly thought. *Sometimes there's nothing better than a hamburger, and the recipe I got from the manager of a fast food chain in Portland will be perfect tonight. I've got a can of beans, and I'll doctor them up the way Mike likes, so he'll be a happy camper.*

She looked at the monitor of her ringing phone and saw that it was Mike. "Hi," she said. Hope you're not calling to tell me you're going to be late."

"Nope, I'm calling to tell you I'm almost home. Be there in about five minutes. How are all the dogs doing?"

Kelly heard a commotion and looked down the hall where Skyy was running with a roll of toilet paper in her mouth and trailing a long white banner behind her. "Well, other than the fact that Skyy has just discovered how much fun it can be to take a roll of toilet paper from its holder and run with it, they're fine," she said laughing. "I'll let you clean that mess up when you get home, so I can concentrate on fixing dinner."

A few minutes later Mike walked in, looked down the hall and rolled his eyes. "I don't know if your cuteness extends this far," he said to the little ball of fur that was jumping on his legs, begging to be picked up. "Rebel, Lady, you have a little work to do with this one. I have no intention of buying stock in a toilet paper company simply because we have a dog that has to run around the house with a roll of it in her mouth." He walked over to Kelly and lightly kissed her. "So, how was your day?"

"Very interesting. And yours?"

"About the same."

"Any luck on finding the killer?" She paused for a moment. "Mike, those words sound awful. I wonder how many marriages there are when almost the first words one spouse says to the other is 'any luck on finding the killer?' I can't believe that's the first thing I asked you."

"I can believe it. It seems we're always in the wrong place at the wrong time, but in answer to your question, no, I didn't have any luck finding the killer. I'll tell you all about my day, but first I need to change clothes and pick up toilet paper. I'll be back in a minute," he said setting Skyy down on the floor. He walked down the hall, followed by Skyy and Rebel. Lady opted to stay with Kelly.

"Thanks, girl. I was beginning to feel unappreciated." She set out the ingredients for the special burgers, put the cast iron grill on the range, and then poured a can of beans into a small saucepan. She added some brown sugar, barbecue sauce, and a few diced onions to the beans. Kelly poured each of them a glass of wine and set the table. Mike returned in a few minutes dressed in a t-shirt and jeans.

She handed him a glass of wine and said, "Could you believe the coffee shop when you were there? It was absolutely standing room only from the time I opened to the time I closed. Rumors were flying, but no one seems to know much about the murder or letting the dogs out of their kennels. What did you find out from the manager?"

"Nothing much. She's still pretty much in shock over the fact that her boss was murdered, and the dogs were let out. We tried to figure out who would have had access to the kennel area. As you know, there are a lot of individual kennels in the big building where the kennels are located. There are four doors that lead into it, so we figure one of those was probably left unlocked by a kennel employee. I asked Sandy if she knew of anyone who would like to see the kennel get bad publicity, and she couldn't think of anyone."

"Did she mention the people Noelle told me about?"

"Yes, she was very aware of the situation with the pit bull guy and the Yorkie woman, but didn't think either one of them was capable of committing murder or letting all the dogs out."

"What about disgruntled employees? Any leads there?"

"Not really. She's the one who hired them and thinks they're all pretty solid. Sandy did mention she didn't particularly care for one of them, a young man named Ricky Anderson. She said her boss, Mary Barnes, had insisted she hire him. She told Sandy that she and the boy's father had been an item at one time, and she hired him as a favor to his father."

"What does he do there?"

"He cleans the kennels and the grounds. I talked to him, and I don't think he has a lot going on upstairs. Actually, having known Mary over the years, I'm kind of surprised she did hire him."

"Hmmm. How old is he?"

"I think he's about nineteen or so. Why?"

"That would make him about the same age as Madison and Brandon. I wonder if they went to school with him. Maybe I should call Madison tomorrow and ask her."

"All right, since she's your employee you can ask her, but that's it. I don't want you talking to him or investigating anything about him, nothing, and I mean zilch, zero, nada. Is that understood?"

"Of course, Mike. You know I wouldn't get involved in one of your cases if you didn't want me to. I just thought one of them might have a little information about him."

"Right, Kelly, right. Why do I think you already know more about this case than I do?"

"Well, you know how things just seem to kind of happen to me. It seems like a couple of things happened to me today that sort of fall into that category."

"I'm sure they did, Kelly. I'm sure they did," he said, raising his eyebrows, "Would you care to tell me what things kind of happened to you today?"

"Of course. I thought you'd never ask."

"Don't push it, Kelly. You're already skating on very thin ice here."

"Well, here's the thing, Mike. I heard about a dog show that started out at the fairgrounds this afternoon, and I thought I'd see what a dog show was like. It was the luckiest thing I went because..."

She told him about her conversation with Jack Powell and the conversation she'd overheard about Lisa and Duchess. When she was finished talking, she asked, "So, what do you think?"

"I think you lead a charmed life. You just happened to be in the places where you'd talk to and overhear conversations from two of the people who hated Mary Barnes. That is a little too much coincidence for me. It could only happen to you. Did you see any other breeds?"

"Well, no. Since Noelle told me that Jack specialized in pit bulls and Lisa had a Yorkie, I thought I'd start with those two. After my success there, I didn't feel I needed to go anywhere else. Oh wait, I did take a peek into the grooming room." She told him what she had seen there.

"I love our dogs," Mike said, "but murdering because of one? That seems like a very far stretch, but I'm beginning to think I'm wrong from what you're telling me. Sounds like there's a lot of money and ego tied up in these dog shows and champion dogs, and both of those things can sure be the basis for a murder."

"Have you gotten a coroner's report yet?"

"Glad you mentioned it. There was a call from the coroner when I was talking to you just before I got home. I'll check it out after dinner, speaking of which, what are we having tonight?"

"One time when I was in Portland I was really pressed for time, and I stopped at a fast food restaurant. You know they're generally not my favorite kind of restaurant, but the hamburger I had there was hands down the best I'd ever had in my life. I told the young woman behind the counter that I'd like to speak to the manager, and I asked him if he could share the recipe. He told me it was a secret recipe, and he couldn't give it to me. I'm not too proud about it, but I took a twenty-dollar bill out of my purse and told him I'd really appreciate it if he could give me the recipe, and he did."

"Kelly, that shocks me. That is so unlike you."

"Wait until you taste this burger. It was worth every penny of the twenty dollars I spent."

"Well, with an intro like that, bring it on!"

When Mike finished the last bite of his burger he said, "I would gladly have given the manager fifty dollars for the recipe for that burger. Easily the best I've ever had, and you know how I love the special way you fix those beans. I think the first time I had them was at the coffee shop."

"It was, and as simple as they are, they're still one of the best sellers, particularly on an overcast winter day. Why don't you go listen to what the coroner has to say while I clean up the dishes? Actually, before you do that you might want to get Skyy off of the couch and take her outside. I have never allowed Rebel or Lady to get up on the furniture, other than our bed, and I sure don't want to start now."

A few minutes later Mike walked into the kitchen, Skyy next to him, wagging her tail.

Kelly put the last of the dishes in the dishwasher and turned to him. "What did the coroner have to say?"

"Mary died from being hit on the head with a blunt instrument."

"Did he say what the instrument was?"

"No, he couldn't tell. He didn't think it was from a gun handle, and he said it seemed to be more like from a hammer or something heavy like that. From where she was hit, he thinks she must have been facing her killer. There was nothing to indicate she was hit from behind."

"I wonder if when the dogs were let out she surprised the person who let them out, and she was just in the wrong place at the wrong time."

"If that's true, she really was in the wrong place at the wrong time. If that theory is correct, the person must have realized she'd seen him or her let the dogs out, and so that person killed Mary in order to conceal his or her identity."

"Mike, was there any indication of bad blood between the manager and Mary?"

"Not that I could tell. She seemed to be genuinely devastated by Mary's death. I really don't think she knows anything. Why do you ask?"

"I was just wondering if there was any resentment on her part for Mary allowing the Pit Bull Sanctuary group to rent from her, because remember, it was one of those pit bulls who severely injured her dog."

"No. I'd completely rule her out. From what she told me, it looks like someone didn't shut the gate properly, and the dog got out."

"Well, it is strange that at the same time and at two different locations gates or doors weren't securely closed."

"I see what you're saying, but I honestly think it was just a coincidence and nothing more."

"Okay, but I know how you feel about coincidences. You always say you don't believe in them. What are your plans for tomorrow? Sounds like you've pretty much found out all you can from the people at the kennel."

"It sounds naïve, but I'm hoping someone who knows something will call me with a lead. It's been in the papers and on the news. The news people and the papers specifically said if anyone had information regarding the case to call my office, and they posted my phone number. I'm hoping it helps. There's no point in going back to the kennel. I've interviewed everyone who works there. Plus, there are a couple of other cases that need my attention. Going to Cuba set me back a bit, and although I've got an increased workload right now, I don't regret a moment of that trip."

"Good, because even with the murder we solved while we were in Cuba, it was a great vacation."

"Kelly," Mike said as he raised his eyebrows, "just because things kind of fell in place in Cuba, and you helped a bit in solving a murder, don't get any ideas about becoming involved in this one."

"Of course not, Mike, that's your area. I've just been a little lucky."

"Well, I know it probably doesn't do any good to ask, but it will make me feel better. Please promise me you won't do anything else on my case."

"You've got it, Sheriff," she said, mentally crossing her fingers behind her back.

CHAPTER FIFTEEN

"See you this afternoon," Kelly said to Mike the next morning as he left for his office. "I plan on being here most of the day playing dutiful housewife. There's a pile of laundry I need to get to, and the house and yard need a little attention. Go get the bad guys."

"Can't promise I'll get them, but I'll sure try. I'll probably give you a call later on and see how this group is doing," he said, bending down and petting Skyy who was intent on untying Mike's shoe by pulling on his shoelace. "Good luck with this one."

Kelly spent the next few hours doing household work and watering the plants and potted flowers. She looked at her watch and thought surely Madison would be up by now. Kelly knew that Saturdays were usually sleep-in days for young people. Madison was in her late teens and in addition to being a student at the local cosmetology school, she worked part-time for Kelly at the coffee shop. Kelly well remembered when her son and daughter, Cash and Julia, were teen-agers. It was never a good idea for anyone to call the house before noon on the weekends. She picked up her cell phone and punched in Madison's phone number. "Hi, Kelly," the voice on the other end said.

"Good morning, or early afternoon, Madison. Do you have a moment?"

"I have plenty of time. I was just doing some homework, although now that I'm almost through with school, there's not much of it. It's more of a hands-on thing."

"This won't take long. I'm wondering if you know a young man named Ricky Anderson. He's about your age, and I thought you might have gone to high school with him."

Madison was quiet for a few moments. "Yes, I remember him. He was always kind of a loner and didn't have many friends." She laughed and said, "Not that I did either, but I've changed a lot in the last couple of years. From what I hear, I'm not so sure Ricky has."

"What do you mean by that?"

"Well, he was expelled from high school. I guess his father was really angry about it. He didn't work or do anything for a long time. I heard his father threatened to throw him out of the house if he didn't go in the Army or get a job. I understand he's working at the Doggie Love Kennel. Oh, Kelly, that's where you boarded your dogs, and that's where the owner was recently killed, right?"

"Right on all accounts. Tell me a little more about him. Why was he expelled?"

"Remember when Roxie's son was buying marijuana from some guy out at Brandon's dad's ranch and selling it to some of the kids at school?"

"Of course. How could I forget? There had been speculation for a long time that his father was growing it on his ranch. Why do you ask?"

"Roxie's son was small potatoes compared to Ricky. He was very involved in buying it and selling it to the students. Problem was, he used most of his profits, if you know what I mean."

"I assume you mean he was actively smoking marijuana."

"That might be the understatement of the year. One day he showed up for class with bloodshot and dilated eyes and everyone knew he was stoned. Our history teacher called the principal's office and then escorted him there. He didn't trust Ricky to go there by himself. The principal expelled him that day. I guess he did a locker search, and it was jammed with the stuff. I've seen him around town a few times since he left school, but that's about it. Actually Brandon and I were just talking about him the other day. Brandon told me he'd heard that Ricky's father was going to give him $5,000 if he could stay on the job at Doggie Love for a year."

"That's a lot of money to a young person or anyone else for that matter. Why do you think his father made a deal like that with him?"

"Ricky's a loser. He's never been successful at anything he's done. I think his father wanted him to try and understand the concept that if he stuck with something, he could be successful. You know, kind of a teaching lesson. I don't think he even got his GED. He's just a high-school dropout cleaning out dog kennels. I can ask Brandon about him if you'd like me to and see if he knows anything more. Brandon came home from college for the weekend."

"No, I think you've given me enough information about Ricky. One more question. Any chance he's still doing drugs?"

Madison was quiet for a long time. "Kelly, I really don't like to spread rumors, but I have heard he's moved up a step from marijuana, and now he's doing heroin."

"In a sleepy little town like Cedar Bay? You've got to be kidding."

"I wish I was. It's kind of the in drug now, and if you have the money, it's available. Don't pass that on. It was just a rumor I heard."

"I'm sorry to hear that about Ricky. I've never even met the kid, but it sounds like his life is over. If he's involved with heroin, has no degree, and can't get a job other than what his dad gets for him, doesn't sound like he's got much of a future."

"Trust me, he doesn't."

"Thanks for taking the time to fill me in, Madison. Go back to your studies. I'll see you Monday morning. Have a nice weekend," Kelly said, ending the call.

She stood for a moment with the phone in her hand, not quite sure what to do with the information Madison had given her. *I wonder if the kennel manager, Sandy, knows about his drug use, or if Mary knew. Maybe she confronted Ricky, and he killed her. Okay, that's a pretty far stretch based on a rumor. Guess I'll have to go to the kennel and meet him. I can always say I can't find Lady's dog tag and wondered if it came loose when she was staying there. While I'm there I'd also like to meet Sandy. I always dealt with Mary when I boarded the dogs there.*

She walked into the bedroom to change clothes and noticed that Skyy was chewing on something. She walked over to the puppy, looked down and said, "Skyy, those are my reading glasses. How did you get them?"

Skyy wagged her tail while Kelly took the glasses away from her. Kelly looked over at the nightstand and saw that the lamp had been moved, and a tissue was shredded on the floor next to the nightstand.

She walked over to it and was sure that Skyy had jumped up on the nightstand, pulled the tissue and glasses off of it, and moved the lamp in the process. She said in a very firm voice, "No, No, Skyy. Bad dog." She slapped the nightstand for emphasis. "No nightstand." Skyy continued to wag her tail.

I'd forgotten how curious puppies are about everything. Think she's definitely a new soul. Lady never did anything like this, and Rebel was already grown when I got him. I hope her cuteness makes up for what I feel may be a few long months. Of course, that's assuming that Mike says we can keep her, but I have a feeling she's here to stay.

CHAPTER SIXTEEN

Kelly parked her minivan in the kennel parking lot and walked over to the door marked "Office." When she opened it she was immediately greeted by a young woman who asked, "May I help you?"

"Yes, I'm Kelly Reynolds. I boarded my dogs, Lady and Rebel, here while my husband and I were in Cuba. I picked them up the day all the dogs had been let out of their kennels by someone. Lady's dog tag is missing, and I'm wondering if you've found it."

"Of course, Mrs. Reynolds. Forgive me for not recognizing you. I'm Sandy Reston, the manager of Doggie Love Kennels. I know Mary usually took care of you. No one has turned in a dog tag, but I'll certainly keep an eye out for it."

"By the way, Sandy, I heard you recently had a horrible experience when your dog was attacked by one of the pit bulls from the Pit Bull Sanctuary. How's your dog doing?"

"She's doing as well as can be expected, but she's still at Dr. Simpson's. It was pretty scary. I still don't understand how it happened. Someone evidently didn't make sure the gate leading to the area where the pit bulls were located was secured. I had to rush Mickey to the vet, and she had emergency surgery. The person who saw what happened had the sense to turn on the hose we use to water the plants and squirt a stream of water on the pit bull to get him to let go of her leg. Dr. Simpson said if the dog hadn't released Mickey's leg, there was a good chance she would have lost it. It's going to cost me a fortune."

"Doesn't the kennel have insurance for things like that? I would think a dog fight among dogs staying at the kennel wouldn't be a particularly uncommon occurrence."

"Yes and no. You see, the pit bulls were not really part of the kennel. They were actually on property that was being leased to the Pit Bull Sanctuary. The Doggie Love Kennel insurance didn't apply to them. What happened was pretty awful, and Mary didn't make it any easier."

"Why?" Kelly asked. "What happened?"

"When I returned from the vet's and told her what happened, the only thing she said was something like, 'Gee, that's too bad.' She had a real soft spot in her heart for the pit bulls. We'd argued before about having pit bulls on the property. I told her our customers would be very angry if anything happened because pit bulls were on the premises.

"I'm not a lawyer," Kelly said, "but it does seem Mary would have had some exposure to liability if anything happened to dogs that were being kenneled here, and the owners weren't made aware that pit bulls were on the premises. A lot of people don't like the breed."

"I know. I asked her if the kennel would pay Mickey's vet bill, and she told me no, that something like that wasn't covered under the kennel's insurance policy. Then I asked her if that was the case, would she personally pay the vet bill, because my dog had been attacked on her property."

"She told me no. Mary insinuated Mickey must have done something to aggravate the pit bull, and she told me she was not responsible for it. I told her how angry my husband was about the incident, because Mickey's pretty much his dog. It didn't help he was in New York on business when it happened, and I had to tell him what happened to Mickey over the phone. He took a red eye flight home that night."

"What a shame. I know how I'd feel if that had happened to one of my dogs."

"Not only was my husband mad," Sandy continued, "he told me if I didn't quit working here he was going to divorce me. I was hoping it was just a spur of the moment thing said in anger. My husband's a lawyer, and he told me Mary was responsible for what happened. He said that if it had been a paying customer's dog, the customer would have sued Mary because ultimately it was her responsibility to make sure that the pit bulls were separated from the dogs that were boarded at the kennel. He thought it was pretty fraudulent that she didn't tell clients about the presence of pit bulls on the property. In her defense, Mary always thought she could keep the pit bulls separate from the paying customers' dogs. It turned out she was wrong."

"Did you agree with your husband and quit?"

"Yes, I gave my two weeks' notice, and then Mary was murdered a couple of days later. My husband said since she'd gotten the pit bulls off the property he would give me a two-week grace period to leave the kennel. I was in the process of finding a replacement when she was killed. Now, everything's up in the air. I don't even know if the kennel will remain in business."

"How did Mary take it when you gave your notice to her?"

"Not well. She said my husband was overreacting and being ridiculous about the whole thing. Mary said he was just some neurotic lawyer, which I have to tell you, didn't sit well with me. She said it was bad enough she had to get rid of the pit bulls that needed foster homes, but I was really adding insult to injury by quitting. She was very angry and yelled at me, saying there was absolutely no reason for me to quit. She told me she didn't have time to train someone new."

"Well, I don't agree with how she handled everything, but I suppose there is some sense to what she said about there not being a reason to quit once the pit bulls were gone."

"They may be gone, and she may be dead, but I have a huge vet bill I still have to pay. My husband has no idea how much it is. He's going to be even angrier than he has been when he finds out. He felt it was kind of rightful justice that someone murdered Mary. I know how he feels. Because of her, I nearly lost our dog and my husband. And people thought she was such a nice person. I wonder what they'd think if I told them the real truth about her. At least the people who presently have their dogs here won't have to worry about something terrible happening to their dogs like what happened to mine."

"Thanks for taking the time to tell me all of this," Kelly said. "If you don't mind, I'd like to walk through the building and see if I can spot Lady's tag. I know it's a long shot, but I'm kind of sentimental about it. My husband gave it to me as a present, and its real silver. Probably doesn't have any value since it's engraved with Lady's name and our address and phone number, but it has value to me."

"Of course, Mrs. Reynolds. Feel free to look around. I'll mention it to the other employees and give you a call if we find anything. Your number's in the dogs' files. Excuse me, but I really do need to get back to work."

"Of course, and again, thanks for your time." Kelly walked out of the office and down a row of kennels, looking for the purportedly lost dog tag which was safely at home hanging from Lady's collar.

CHAPTER SEVENTEEN

For the next few minutes Kelly walked up and down the rows of kennels making it look as if she was searching for the lost dog tag. She saw a door and stepped outside. She remembered Mary telling her that she'd hired a contractor to build a lake, so the dogs that liked water would have a place to swim, but she'd never taken the time to look at it. The lake was much larger than she thought it would be, and obviously it could accommodate a lot of dogs at the same time.

Wow! That must have cost a fortune. No wonder she charged so much to board the dogs.

She noticed a young man sitting next to the lake with his back to her, smoking a cigarette and coughing. She'd never met Ricky Anderson, but the young man seemed to be about the right age. She walked over to him.

"Hi, I'm Kelly Reynolds. I assume you work here," she said. He turned to face her and she took in his puffy eyes and the dark circles under them. Even though it was a warm day, he was wearing a heavy long-sleeved red flannel shirt buttoned up to his neck.

Odd he'd be wearing a long-sleeved shirt on a beautiful day like today. Wonder if the rumors Madison heard are true. Maybe he's trying to hide track marks on his arms from using heroin.

He slowly shuffled to his feet and threw his cigarette on the ground, grinding it out with the heel of his shoe. "I'm Ricky Anderson. What are you doing out here? Clients ain't supposed to come out here. Jes' the employees and the dogs."

"My dogs were recently boarded here. One of them lost her ID tag and I'm trying to find it, but this is a big place, and so far I haven't had any luck. I assume you work here."

"Yeah, might call me the do-what-no-one-else-wants-to-do man," he said in a voice tinged with bitterness.

"That's kind of an intriguing job description."

"Might be intriguing, but that's all it is. I've only got a couple more months to go, and then I'm outta here."

"I take it this is not going to be a career for you."

"Ya' got that right. This ain't a career for nobody. I'm just serving time here. Kinda like a jail only I get paid. Two more months, and I hit the big payday."

"I'm sorry, but I have no idea what you're talking about."

"Nah, ya' probably wouldn't. Promised my dad I'd work here for a year. Time's almost up. Can't happen too fast for me 'cause once it does my old man promised to pay me five grand."

"That's a lot of money. I understand the owner recently died. Is that going to affect your time here?"

"Dunno. If they close it down, yeah, probably will. Old bat had it coming, though. Don't know of anyone here that's real sorry she's gone. Didn't treat none of us too good."

"My dogs always seemed to like it here, and I never had any problems, but I guess a couple of people did."

"Yeah, kinda funny. One of them pit bulls got out and got in some fancy little Yorkie's kennel. Had himself a good time," he said laughing. "Course he had to leave a few weeks later when one of 'em bit Sandy's dog real bad. Mary wasn't too happy 'bout all that kinda bad stuff goin' down at her kennel, I can tell you that."

"I imagine she wouldn't have been. How did the pit bull get out and get in the Yorkie's kennel?"

"Dunno. Guess someone didn't make sure the gates and doors were closed," he said, looking off into the distance. "Can't be too careful 'bout stuff like that. Matter of fact the old biddy kinda insinuated I mighta done it." He laughed. "Didn't do it, but it sure musta been somethin' to see."

"Where are you going when you're finished working here? Do you have another job lined up?"

"Naw. Headin' south. Looking to have me a little fun in the sun. Mexico's been callin' to me. I'm tired of it always bein' foggy and cold here. May be sunny today, but I'm still cold. Need to go somewhere warm."

Hmmmm. I've always heard that someone who's using heroin can't get warm. Hate to think it, but something is definitely not right with this boy. Knowing Mary, I find it hard to believe she hired him.

"Gotta get back to the kennels. Was jes' takin' a little break from sloppin' 'em out. Gets real old real quick and even worse when someone's always tellin' ya' it ain't bein' done the right way. Don't miss the old broad, that's fer sure."

"Nice talking to you, Ricky. I was hoping to find Lady's dog tag somewhere around here. Being a Lab, she loved the water, so I thought maybe she'd lost it out here, but it doesn't look like it. If you find it, would you give it to Sandy? She said she'd call me if someone found it."

"Sure, but don't trust everything she says."

"What do you mean?"

"Nothin', nothin' at all. Jes' things aren't always what they seem to be." With that he turned and walked through the door into the main building, mop in hand.

I wonder if he knows something about Mary's death. What is going on here? This is all very strange.

CHAPTER EIGHTEEN

Kelly walked into the house, greeted the two big dogs, and unlatched Skyy's kennel. She didn't trust the puppy to be running loose in the house when she was gone, so Skyy had to be confined in her kennel while Kelly was away from the house. "Time to commune with nature. The three of you can spend a little time outside while I figure out what to fix for dinner. It's a beautiful afternoon, and you might as well enjoy it. We don't get too many of them living this close to the Oregon coast."

She walked into the kitchen, opened the refrigerator, and decided that Saturday night was a perfect night for serving Rock Cornish game hens with an apricot stuffing.

Hmm, asparagus with hollandaise and a wedge salad will be perfect accompaniments, she thought. *Even if Mike didn't catch any bad guys today, he'll be happy with dinner. Plus, I've got enough time to make that brie and egg strata he loves for breakfast tomorrow morning. We can enjoy breakfast while I do the Sunday crossword puzzle, and he decides if there's anything in the newspaper I need to know about, or if it's just the usual "if it bleeds, it leads" type of news.*

She spent the next hour assembling the strata and making the stuffing for the game hens as well as the orange sauce she liked to spoon over the hens just before serving them. While she was cooking, Kelly became aware that it was very quiet in the back yard,

81

unnaturally quiet. She walked over to the door and saw all three dogs patiently sitting in front of the door, waiting for their dinners.

The dogs had just finished eating when Mike opened the door and said, "Okay everyone, I'm home. I know you all missed me, right?"

"Right," Kelly said as she walked over and hugged him. Skyy raced over and sat in front of him whining and demanding to be picked up. He obliged and petted the other two dogs at the same time. "This family is growing. I'm not sure I have enough gas in my tank for all of you," he laughed.

"Sheriff, I don't think your deputies want to hear you say that. I'd keep talk like that right here at home. Think your deputies are more interested in whether or not you're going to catch the bad guys."

"You're probably right," he said, setting Skyy down. She immediately tried to jump up on Rebel who looked at her and growled. She sat back on her haunches, head cocked, trying to figure out what she'd done to earn the growl, but Kelly and Mike both noticed she didn't jump on the big boxer again.

"Sit down and relax, Mike. Seriously, did you have any luck today with the Barnes murder?"

"I wish I could say I did, but absolutely nothing new has developed. I know the pit bull guy and the Yorkie woman both have motives, but I'm having a hard time seeing either one of them as a killer. As much as I hate to ask, did you call Madison and find out anything about Ricky Anderson?"

"Yes, not only did I find out about him, I met him."

"Kelly, that wasn't part of the agreement. You were only going to find out what Madison knew about him, period."

"Uh-huh," she said handing him a glass of wine and taking a seat across the table from him. "Actually, what I found out is kind of interesting." She filled him in on what Madison had told her about

Ricky as well as her impression of him after she met him.

"I'm gathering from what Madison said and from your tone of voice, you think he could be a possible suspect. Would I be right?" he asked.

"Well, yes. He clearly didn't like Mary, he doesn't like his job, and he was almost giggling about the pit bull getting out. Something is not right with that guy. I think the rumors Madison heard about him are probably true, which means he's heavily into drugs. His eyes, the fact he wore a long-sleeve shirt completely buttoned up, and his cough are all signs of heroin use. Before I went out to the kennel I searched the Internet to see what it said about observing heroin use in someone. All three of those signs were listed as possible indications that a person is using heroin."

"Of course, and if it's on the Internet it must be the truth, right?" he asked in a teasing voice.

"I recognize that tone of voice," she said, "but I looked at a bunch of different sites, so I think I can say that with those identifiers he probably is on something, and most likely, it's heroin."

"Let me play devil's advocate for a moment. If he is on something, would he have it together enough to be able to commit murder?"

"I don't know. For that matter we still don't know which came first, the chicken or the egg. In other words, was Mary killed before the dogs were let out, or did she see someone letting them out and then that someone killed her?"

"I agree. The answer to that question has really been bothering me."

"Mike, I hate to add to your trouble, but I think I have a couple more suspects for you."

"What's this 'you think you have a couple more suspects' Kelly?

As I recall, we had an agreement that this was my case, and you would not get involved in it. I'm getting the distinct impression you're getting involved, seriously involved."

"Don't get up on your high horse, Mike. I've been pretty lucky in the past. Cut me some slack for a few moments and just hear me out."

"Like I have a choice," he grumbled.

"I think you need to take a long look at the manager of Doggie Love Kennel, Sandy Reston."

"I know you'll tell me, but I'll play dumb and ask why?"

"She has a motive, actually several. Number one, her dog was viciously attacked because of Mary's affinity for the pit bulls. Number two, neither the kennel's insurance nor Mary would pay the hefty vet bill for her seriously injured dog, and number three, her husband threatened to divorce her because of the incident. Evidently she and Mary had argued about the pit bulls being on the property several times before. It was pretty clear to me there was no love lost between the two of them. And lastly, Ricky indicated that maybe Sandy isn't quite what she appears to be.

"I'm not sure I'm ready to take into account the word of a drug addict when I'm looking for a killer."

"I have no idea what's important and what's not. I'm just telling you some things you probably need to consider. Think about it while I put the finishing touches on dinner. Even if you aren't happy about the way the case is going I know you're going to be happy with what I'm about to serve you, plus I made the brie and egg strata that you like so much for breakfast tomorrow morning. You can read the paper and enjoy the day."

"Shall I close my eyes while you surprise me with dinner?"

"No. You can admire the gorgeous stuffed Rock Cornish game

hen you're about to be served along with a special warm orange sauce, green beans with hollandaise, and a wedge salad. As they say in France, *bon appetit!*

CHAPTER NINETEEN

On the short drive to the coffee shop on Monday morning, Kelly thought about how lovely the day before had been. A leisurely breakfast, Mike helping her with the last of the neglected household chores, catching up on e-mails, and long conversations with both Julia and Cash. Julia filled her in on what was happening at their ranch in Calico Gold, while Cash shared some thrilling news with her.

He told her his tour of duty in Iraq would be over in just a few weeks, and his new assignment was going to be at Guantanamo Bay in Cuba. He was really excited to be stationed there. He saved the best news for last, when he told her he had some time off between assignments and would be visiting Mike and her in a few weeks. The very thought of seeing him brought a smile to her face. Nearly every day while he'd been in Iraq Kelly had worried she'd get a phone call telling her that her wonderful son had become a statistic. She prayed he could make it safely to the end of his tour and hopefully, never have to return to Iraq.

When she arrived at the pier where the coffee shop was located she got the dogs out of the minivan and as usual, Roxie, Charlie, and Madison walked up to the door just as she was opening it. The three of them had worked for Kelly for quite a while and each went about their morning duties in preparation for what promised to be another busy day. Whenever there was an unsolved mystery in the small town, and in the recent past there had been quite a few mysteries including several murders, the townspeople gathered at Kelly's Koffee Shop hoping to find out something about these crimes. Usually what they found out was nothing more than a rumor, but it gave them something to do, and in a town as small as Cedar Bay diversions from the ordinary were very welcome.

"Madison, would you give me a hand with the groceries that are in my minivan? I had to restock and could use a little help carrying them in."

"Of course, plus it will give me a chance to tell you what I learned from Brandon about Ricky."

"Well, you definitely have my attention," she said as they walked out to her minivan. "By the way, I met him Saturday, and although I know what you told me about his drug use wasn't based on facts, after meeting with him I would have to agree with the rumors."

"That's what I was going to tell you. I talked to Brandon last night and mentioned Ricky to him. He told me he'd been at a party Friday night when he'd come back from college, and Ricky was there. Everybody was surprised when he walked in the door, because none of them had invited him. In fact, the people there never had anything to do with him when they were in high school, and certainly not after graduation. They all thought it was pretty strange."

"So what did he do? Just show up?" Kelly asked as she loaded several grocery bags in Madison's arms.

"That seems to be about it. He wasn't there too long. It looks like the drug use is true. Brandon said he was really wasted, and stupid enough that he asked several people who were there if they wanted some good stuff. He told them he had a friend that could always score big and said what this person had was the real deal."

"Did anyone take him up on his offer?"

"Of course not. Brandon said drugs are certainly used where he goes to college, but he doesn't do them, and he told me none of the people who were there Friday night did either. After a little while one of the guys told Ricky he thought it might be a good thing if he left. Several of the other guys stood behind him when he said it. At some level Ricky must have gotten the message, because he left right after the guy told him to."

"That's interesting," Kelly said as they walked back into the coffee shop. "Thanks for telling me. Don't know what I can do with that information, but it seems to confirm the rumors you heard. I probably better tell Mike. He hates drugs and even more, people who sell drugs. From the way Ricky talked, it sounds like he might be selling heroin. Maybe Mike can do something about it. Let me ask you something else, and then we both need to get back to work."

"Sure, what is it?"

"Seems like every time we talk, you mention Brandon. As your Catholic sponsor, should I know something?" she asked, grinning

A few days after Madison had started working at Kelly's Koffee Shop, she'd attended a funeral for Kelly's goddaughter, Amber. After attending the Catholic funeral service, Madison had what some would call a spiritual awakening. Her life completely changed, and she credited her father ending his alcohol abuse, her good grades at cosmetology school, and all the wonderful things that had happened to her because of it and Kelly.

Madison blushed and said, "I like Brandon, and I think he likes me. He knows I've changed since Amber's death, and although I know he was very much in love with her, and had even planned on marrying her, we've both gotten over it. He usually comes home from college about twice a month, and that's when I get to see him. He calls me from school a couple of times a week. Kelly, I don't know if there's any future in it, but I hope so."

"Honey, I hope so too. You both deserve some happiness. I'd be thrilled if you could find it with each other. I like him a lot, and you tell him he better appreciate you, or he'll have to deal with me."

Madison laughed. "Kelly, because of you everything in my life is good. Dad and I have never been closer, and Doc and his wife have been kind of like parents to me since Doc helped dad get sober. In fact, Doc's wife and I have become very close. I'm really, really happy."

"Well, if you're happy, that makes me happy. Enough of this. Please put the groceries away. Charlie can handle the short orders, and I'll start cooking the rest of the stuff. Oh, and Madison, I just want you to know how proud I am of you, and although you say the changes in your life are because of me, that's not true. The changes in your life are because you decided to make something of your life and you definitely did! Now, get started, or we'll both end up crying."

CHAPTER TWENTY

As Kelly was getting ready to lock up for the day, Roxie walked out of the kitchen, untied her apron, and said, "I've been meaning to tell you something all afternoon, but we were so busy I never could find the time to do it."

"What is it?" Kelly asked.

"Well, just after lunch a man came in and wanted to know some information about you."

"Why didn't you tell him I'd be happy to talk to him?"

"I told him I'd get you, but he said no. He just wanted to know a little bit about you, but he asked some things I thought were kind of strange."

"Like what?"

"He wanted to know if you or your husband had discovered who killed Mary Barnes."

"Did he say who he was or why he was asking?"

"No. He said he'd heard you'd solved some crimes in the past and that you'd been asking some questions about the murder out at the

Doggie Love Kennel. That's all I know. Oh, he did ask where you lived."

"You're kidding. What did you tell him?"

"I told him you'd helped your husband solve several criminal cases recently, but I hadn't heard anything about you trying to solve the Mary Barnes case. I also told him I couldn't give out information about where you lived."

"That's really weird. I can tell you this, I don't like it when someone comes snooping around asking questions about me. I wonder who he was."

"I have no idea."

"I'm glad you didn't tell him where I lived. That was a smart decision, Roxie. What did he look like?" Kelly asked.

"He was fairly young, probably about thirty. Of course now that I'm getting older, everyone under forty looks young to me. He was wearing a grey suit, horn-rimmed glasses, and his brown hair was cut pretty short. He had a moustache, and I remember he had beautiful dark blue eyes that it was hard to look away from. I think he might have been a lawyer, because I did mention that you'd probably he happy to talk to him after the noon rush hour. He mentioned something about having to be in court. He didn't order anything. It seems his whole purpose for coming to the coffee shop was to find out what he could about you. I thought it was very strange, so I made a point of watching him when he left. He got in a fairly new silver car, but I don't know the make. I thought you'd want to know. Might want to keep your eyes open."

"Do you think he was from Cedar Bay? I thought you knew pretty much everyone in town."

"I know the townies that have lived here for a long time, but he might be from one of the newer areas. There are a lot of new developments on the south side of town. Come to think of it, no one here at the restaurant greeted him, and if he lived here in town, I'm sure someone would have recognized him. He didn't seem particularly threatening, but all in all it was strange enough to get my attention."

"Thanks, Roxie, I'm sure it was nothing. I don't think I'll even bother to tell Mike. Something like that will just make him nervous. Now get out of here. It's time for you to leave. See you in the morning."

Kelly put Skyy on a leash and turned to Lady and said, "Time to go home." When she put her seat belt on and started her minivan she had a sense she was being watched, and a chill went down the back of her neck. She looked around, but didn't see anyone. On the drive home she kept checking her rear-view mirror to see if she was being followed. She noticed a silver sedan two cars back and debated whether or not to turn onto her street. She wanted to see if it was the man Roxie had told her about and if the car was actually following her. She turned onto her street and carefully watched her rear view mirror. The silver car continued on past the intersection.

I must be jumpy. If it was the guy Roxie was talking about and he wanted to find out where I lived, he probably would have followed me. This is silly, and I'm sure I'm overreacting. I think I'll call Sandy when I get home and see if she's heard anything. I can use the lost ID tag thing again.

"Doggie Love Kennel, how may I help you?" the voice that answered the phone asked.

"This is Kelly Reynolds. I'd like to speak with Sandy Renton."

"Oh, hi Kelly, this is Sandy. I was just getting ready to leave. My husband's picking me up in a few minutes. He's leaving for New York tomorrow, so we thought we'd go out tonight for a nice dinner. There's a new restaurant not too far from where we live, and we've decided to try it out."

"What's the name of it? Because of the coffee shop, I know most of the restaurants in the area."

"It's French. I believe the name is *Bon Ami*. I think it means good friend in French."

"It must be very new. I've never heard of it. Where's it located?"

"It's in the Trunsdale Estates shopping center. We bought a home in that area several months ago."

"Isn't that one of the new developments south of town?"

"Yes. We just love it. My husband's a lawyer for one of the lumber companies and travels a lot. He feels much better knowing we live in a gate-guarded community, and thinks it's much safer for me when he's away."

"I can understand that," Kelly said. "Enjoy your dinner. I'm just calling to see if you've had any luck finding Lady's ID tag."

"Sorry, absolutely none. I've told all of the people who work here, but no one knows anything about it. Oh, I can see my husband's car turning the corner. He calls it grey, but I think it's more of a silver color. I'll call you if we find Lady's tag. Bye."

Kelly ended the call and sat for a few moments, deep in thought. *He drives a grey-silver car, lives in a new development south of town, and he's a lawyer. Those are an awful lot of coincidences, and Mike's made a believer out of me about coincidences. I wonder if the man who was in the coffee shop today is her husband. I also wonder if it was his car I saw earlier. If it was him, and if it was his car, why would he be following me? I can't think of any reason. This is really strange. Maybe I should tell Mike.*

CHAPTER TWENTY-ONE

Later that afternoon Kelly caught herself constantly looking out the kitchen window at the street to see if there was a grey or silver car driving by the house. The fact that there wasn't made her wonder all the more if the man who had been at the coffee shop was Sandy's husband.

Her attention was diverted by a furry whirlwind in the form of Skyy who went flying by Kelly's feet with what looked like a pair of glasses in her mouth. Skyy ran down the hall and into the bathroom where she stopped and began chewing on the earpiece. "Oh no you don't. Come here Skyy," Kelly yelled, as she ran after the puppy. "Those are Mike's, and he is not going to be happy about you chewing on them." She reached down and took the glasses away from the puppy who was clearly unaware of why she shouldn't have taken the glasses and chewed on them when the ear smells on them were so good!

Kelly heard the front door open and Mike's deep voice resonating through the house. "Hey everybody, I'm home. Kelly, where are you?"

"In the bathroom taking care of a little puppy business. Skyy decided your reading glasses would be fun to chew on, and I had to take them away from her."

Mike walked into the bathroom and looked at Skyy. "How did she get those? They were on my desk when I left this morning."

"I have no idea how she got them, but I would venture a guess that she stood up on her back legs with her paws on top of the desk and saw them. They proved to be irresistible to her, and since I'd never told her they were off limits, she decided to take them from the desk. Bet you didn't tell her either."

Mike reached down and gently petted Skyy. "That is unacceptable behavior, little one. Glasses are definitely not for puppies." He stood up and kissed Kelly lightly on the cheek. "How was the start of the week at the coffee shop? Rumors still flying?"

"Yes, and I've been debating whether or not I should tell you something," she said as they walked down the hall and into their bedroom. He unstrapped his gun and began changing clothes.

His muffled voice came from the closet. "Kelly, if you're debating whether or not you should tell me something, you absolutely should. What is it?"

"Let's go sit down in the great room and watch the sun set on the bay. It's always so beautiful to see the colors of the sky as they begin to blend with the ocean. I know it's silly, but I almost think I can see Hawaii when it happens. You know this is my favorite time of the day. Sunset over the bay and a glass of wine. What's not to like? Life doesn't get much better than that!"

"Lady, your wants are pretty simple. Give me some time to wash up, and I'll join you in a couple of minutes."

A few minutes later after they'd watched the sun fade into the ocean, Mike said, "Okay, time to tell me what it is that you were debating about telling me."

"Mike, I really don't know where to go with this, but before I tell you I want you to promise me one thing."

"What's that?"

"Promise me you won't go all macho man on me and try and protect me."

"Kelly, what in the devil have you gotten yourself into this time? I'll promise you I won't go all macho man as you put it, but I can't promise you I won't try and protect you."

She took a deep breath and told him about her conversation with Roxie and her subsequent conversation with Sandy. She mentioned they both had said the man in question drove a silver/grey car, and that she'd seen one when she was leaving the coffee shop and felt spooked. When she finished, she asked, "So what do you think it all means?"

Mike was quiet for several moments and then began to speak. "Kelly, I'm not certain what to think. I've never met the man. I have no information that would tell me whether or not it was Sandy's husband who asked questions about you and the coffee shop, and I certainly don't know if you were being followed. What I am certain of is I don't like some man asking where you live, and from what you're telling me, he didn't seem like someone who was simply interested in an attractive woman."

"Thanks for the compliment, but I agree. I'm glad Roxie didn't tell whoever he was where I lived. The whole thing kind of creeps me out. I found myself checking to make sure the doors were locked, and I even looked out the window a number of times to see if there was a grey or silver car driving by on our street."

"Kelly, did you say anything to Sandy that would make her think you suspected her in connection with the murder of Mary Barnes?"

"No. You and I talked about it the other night, but that was as far as I've gone with it. When I went to the Doggie Love Kennel on Saturday, it was under the guise that Lady had lost her dog tag. If you remember, I told her it was silver and had been a gift from you. I told you I was a little suspicious of her but no, I haven't told anyone else.

"Maybe she looked at Rebel's and Lady's files and saw that I owned Kelly's Koffee Shop and was married to you, and she might have told her husband. I suppose it could have even been Mary who told her I owned a coffee shop. I'm really going out on a limb here, but maybe Sandy was the one who committed the murder and she told her husband. If that's true, he could be worried that I suspect her, and he wants to get rid of me in order to protect his wife. I know this all sounds pretty far-fetched."

"None of what you've just told me would fly in a criminal justice course called Suspect 101. As a matter of fact, if any of my deputies told me they suspected someone had committed a crime based on evidence that flimsy, I wouldn't go along with it. Tell you what, let me do some investigating and see what I can find out about this guy. In the meantime, I think I'll take Lady with me to work and you take Rebel and Skyy. From what I've seen so far of Skyy, she's got a long way to go before she can provide you with any meaningful protection, but Rebel has always watched out for you, and I'd feel better if he was with you. Now, what can I do to help you get dinner on the table?"

CHAPTER TWENTY-TWO

Kelly woke up the following morning and remembered she needed to take Skyy to the veterinarian. When she'd called Dr. Simpson and told him she had a new puppy, he'd been adamant that she bring her in and let him examine the puppy even though Mary had taken Skyy to him when she'd first gotten the puppy. Kelly decided she'd take Skyy to see him after she closed the coffee shop that afternoon. She looked over at Mike, sleeping peacefully beside her, and blew him a kiss as she got out of bed, dressed, let the dogs out, and put Rebel and Skyy in her minivan.

There was a lull about ten in the morning, so she called Dr. Simpson's office and made an appointment with him for four that afternoon. She closed the coffee shop at 2:45 and had about an hour before Skyy's appointment. She decided to make a couple of the brie and egg stratas like the one she'd made Mike for breakfast on Sunday. They were always a hit with the customers, but they took a little time to prepare.

About the time she finished with the stratas, it was time to head for Dr. Simpson's vet clinic. Rebel wasn't a big fan of the vet, and it always amused Kelly how the big dog would start to quiver and shake whenever she took him to see Dr. Simpson. Rebel seemed to sense he was being taken there to get a shot or that something else would be done to him that he wouldn't like. The big boxer was very happy when Kelly lifted Skyy up from the back seat and left him alone in the minivan with the windows halfway down.

"Hi, Mrs. Reynolds, is this the newest addition to the family? That puppy sure looks familiar," the receptionist said.

"For now," Kelly said. "I'm trying to convince my husband we need to have three dogs. He's really taken with her, but I haven't been able to get a firm commitment from him that three dogs will be okay. I want to make sure Skyy's vaccines and puppy shots are current. She was Mary Barnes' dog, and as you probably heard, she was murdered. Her daughter gave Skyy to me because she knows how much I like dogs, but she was pretty rattled and didn't bring me Skyy's vet records. I figured you'd have a record here, and I wouldn't have to bother her. Poor lady has enough to deal with."

"I agree. It will be in her file. Give me a minute. How are Lady and Rebel doing with her?"

"They've fully accepted her. I have this theory that puppies do better when there's an older dog around that can act as a role model."

"I think you're absolutely right. Looks like she's ready for her Bordatella vaccine. You can put her in room two. Dr. Simpson will be with you shortly."

"Good. I want him to take a look at her and make sure everything is okay. She seems fine to me, but since I don't have any records for her, and I don't want to bother Mary's daughter, I'd appreciate his input."

A few minutes later the chubby affable bearded veterinarian entered the exam room. "Good seeing you Kelly. I think I recognize this new addition to the family."

"Yes, I know you've already met her. Mary Barnes' daughter asked if I'd take her for the present time. When I called to tell you about her, you said I should bring her in to make sure everything was okay with her even though you've examined her before. I just want to be doubly sure, and your receptionist said she was ready for her

Bordatella vaccine."

"No problem. Give me a minute." He picked up the wiggling ball of fur and spent the next few minutes examining her.

There was a knock on the door and the receptionist opened it. "I'm sorry to bother you, Doctor, but Mrs. Collins is on the phone. She sounds hysterical."

"All right. I'll take the call from here. This is getting old. I'm sorry, Kelly, but I probably better take this one. I'll just be a minute," he said as he picked up the phone. "This is Dr. Simpson, how is Duchess doing?"

Kelly could clearly hear Lisa's voice, and agreed with the receptionist, she sounded hysterical. "Doctor, I'm so worried. Duchess doesn't look good. She has a very sad look in her eyes."

The doctor rolled his eyes heavenward. "Mrs. Collins, we've talked about this several times before. You're going to bring Duchess here to the clinic a couple of days before her due date, so if she encounters problems giving birth, I can take care of her. A sad look in her eyes is not something that causes me to be concerned."

Again Kelly could clearly hear Lisa. "Doctor, this is absolutely the worst thing that's ever happened to me. I'm still so angry, and frankly I'm glad that horrible woman was murdered. It serves her right for allowing something like this to happen to my baby. She deserved to die for the pain she's caused me and my precious little Duchess."

"Well, Mrs. Collins, that's a matter of opinion. Try not to worry. Duchess is going to be fine. Dogs are a lot hardier than we give them credit for. I'm with a patient, so I really need to go. We'll make the arrangements for boarding Duchess at the clinic when it's a little closer to her due date." He hung up the phone and turned to Kelly.

"I know how attached people get to their pets, but lately it seems like I've had more than my fair share of them," he said turning back to Kelly.

"I overheard a couple of people talking about her at the dog show at the fairgrounds last Friday," Kelly said. "Evidently one of the other dogs at the Doggie Love Kennel impregnated Duchess. They mentioned that Mrs. Collins was very worried that the dog that did it might have been much larger than Duchess, and it could cause problems for her during the birth process. From what they were saying, it sounds like she was really angry."

"She still is. I understand her concern, but there's nothing she can do about it. We discussed Duchess having an abortion, but Mrs. Collins' personal beliefs stopped her from doing that, and I respect her feelings. It's just a very difficult situation. Mary's kennel has sure had its share of problems lately. Pit bull problems, Duchess' pregnancy, Mary's death, the dogs being released from the kennel, and then the attack on the Reston dog. Poor dog is still recuperating here at the clinic."

"I spoke with Sandy Reston the other day. I understand that it was her husband's dog, and he was quite upset about it."

"That's putting it mildly. He's kind of a strange guy."

"I don't know him. Tell me about him."

CHAPTER TWENTY-THREE

"Kelly, I really don't like to talk about my patients or their owners. I hope you can understand that. Why do you want to know?"

"Doctor, we go back a long way. You know I'm married to the Beaver County Sheriff, and I think you know that I've helped him solve some of the murder cases that have occurred in and around Cedar Bay. The death of Mary Barnes is a very strange case. It seems like there are a lot of people who might have a motive for murdering her. Several of them involve dogs which are probably patients of yours."

"That very thought has been keeping me awake the last few nights."

"If I made a promise to you that I would never tell anyone about any conversation we might have, could you trust me enough to give me your thoughts? I think you could really help us with this investigation."

Dr. Simpson was quiet for several moments, obviously deep in thought. "Kelly, I've known you a long time, and I trust you. I probably would feel better getting this off my chest, but I must insist my name be kept entirely out of anything that might come about as a result of this conversation."

"If it would make you feel better, I won't even tell Mike."

"He seems like a good man, although I've only met him a couple of times. Go ahead and tell him whatever you feel is relevant, but please don't say you heard it from me."

"That's more than fair. I won't use your name as being a source."

"Since I'm the only veterinarian in town, I pretty much know all the dog owners. You know my feelings about Lisa. She was in shock and very, very angry when I confirmed that Duchess was pregnant. Do I think she qualifies as a suspect? I honestly don't know. I suppose she might have been angry enough to commit murder, but I have a hard time seeing her as a killer. I also have a hard time seeing her as the person who let the dogs loose at the kennel."

"That was pretty much my impression as well," Kelly said, "but I have learned that sometimes the one person you don't think is capable of committing murder is actually the one who has committed the murder."

"I'm sure that's true, and you would know more about that than me. I don't know if you know Jack Powell. He's the head of a group called the Pit Bull Sanctuary. He pays me a retainer and brings in various different pit bulls from time to time. He's passionate about the breed, and while I've never known him to be violent, he was furious he had to find another place for the pit bulls after one of them attacked Sandy Reston's dog. He felt he was very lucky to find foster homes for the dogs with almost no notice."

"Actually, I had a long talk with him at the dog show," Kelly said, "and he told me about the incident. He seemed really angry that Mary had made such a quick decision. He felt what she did was unfair to him and the dogs, because it didn't allow him enough time to rent space for them somewhere else."

"Yes, that's true. Now that brings me to the Restons. Evidently Sandy and Mary had disagreed for a long time about the pit bulls being on the premises. When one of the pit bulls savagely attacked

Mickey, the Reston's dog, the situation came to a head. Sandy was furious when she brought her in to me for emergency treatment and ultimately surgery. She told me she was going to have to call her husband and tell him, because the dog was his baby. Sandy said her husband was in New York and would not be happy about it."

"I guess she was lucky the dog didn't lose its leg."

"Very. It was one of the worst injuries I've ever seen. In fact, the dog is still here, even though it happened several days ago. I don't know if he'll ever regain full use of that leg. Her husband comes in daily to see the dog. Sandy might have gotten over it, but her husband definitely hasn't. Quite frankly, if I were to pick one person that might qualify as a leading suspect, I would probably pick Hank."

"I don't know him. Why do you say that?"

"There's not much I can tell you. He's a lawyer for a lumber company, and he travels a lot. When he's gone, I understand Sandy takes their dog with her when she goes to work at Doggie Love Kennel. There's nothing specific I can tell you about him, it's more of a sense that I have about him. He seems to have anger issues."

"Can you give me an example?"

"The one that comes to mind is something that happened several months ago. It was time for his dog to be given her annual Bordetella vaccine. I don't know if you've noticed, but when this building was built, the way to open the front door was inadvertently reversed."

"What do you mean, reversed?"

"Usually the right side of a door swings open. When the contractor built ours, somehow it got reversed, and the left side of the door is the side that swings open."

"I've never noticed it," Kelly said, "but I will on the way out. I'm still a little unclear what this has to do with Mary Barnes' death."

"Sandy and her husband moved here about a year ago, and he brought his dog in to meet me and talk to me about shots, etc. When he opened the door and came in he was furious about the way the door opened. He was so angry he was shaking and told me I should have that door reversed. It seemed overkill to me. What's interesting is that he still gets just as angry over that door every time he comes here. That's what I mean when I say I think he has some anger issues. Seems to me the situation with the front door shouldn't merit that amount of anger."

"I agree. I suppose he could have a motive to commit murder in that his dog was severely injured while she was staying at Doggie Love Kennel, but I do have a problem seeing a young lawyer risking everything by doing something like that."

"Yes, I've considered the same thing, but if someone has severe anger issues, I'm not so sure they think that far ahead. Often it's simply reacting to whatever is in the moment."

"Let me ask you something, Doctor. What's your impression of Sandy Reston?"

"I like Sandy, but I do think she's intimidated by her husband. I told you she was panicked when she brought the dog in after it had been attacked. She seemed to be far more worried about what her husband was going to say than she was about the dog's injury. I found that to be very unusual."

"Doctor Simpson, I just thought of something. I know this is really a leap, but I noticed a big bruise on Sandy's jaw when I talked to her the other day. She was wearing a lot of make-up, and I had a fleeting thought that maybe someone had hit her, and she was trying to cover the bruise up. I have absolutely nothing to base it on."

He was quiet for several moments, and then he said, "I've never put it together, but now that I think about it, I've seen bruises on her several times. One time I commented on a bruise, and she told me she'd tripped on the stairs and fallen. Are you thinking what I'm thinking?"

"Let's put it this way, Doctor. I don't like what I'm thinking."

"Kelly, I'm going to have to go. I'm running late. I feel better after talking to you, but I'm not too sure how valid anything I've said is, or if it will be of any help to you and Sheriff Mike."

"Thanks, Doctor. When I find out something, I'll let you know. Glad you approve of the new little girl."

"I think she's going to be a beauty. Mary was thrilled to get that dog, and with good reason. She'd spent a lot of time researching where to get a dog that she felt could be a champion. Are you planning on showing her or breeding her?"

"I don't think I'd feel very comfortable in that world. We love our dogs, but as pets, not as commodities. Thanks for spending so much time with me. I'll be in touch."

CHAPTER TWENTY-FOUR

Kelly felt unsettled when she left Dr. Simpson's office. She couldn't get the thought out of her mind that Sandy Renton was being abused by her husband. Since Sandy and Hank had only moved to the Cedar Bay area within the past year, she doubted if Sandy had any close friends she could confide in.

Maybe this whole thing is in my mind. I'd like to clear it up once and for all. I need to talk to her and see if there's anything I can do to help her if she's a victim of spousal abuse. Of course, it may be nothing, and if that's the case, the worst that can happen is she'll never talk to me again. Seem to remember some old saying about nothing ventured, nothing gained. I think I'll go out to the kennel right now and talk to her. If she is being abused and something happens to her, I'll never forgive myself if I don't at least try to help.

Kelly drove out to the kennel, pulled the minivan into the kennel parking lot, and partially rolled down the windows so the dogs could get some fresh air. She took a deep breath, swallowed hard, walked over to the office, and opened the door. It was somewhat dark inside, but she was able to make out Sandy sitting at her desk in front of a computer.

Sandy looked up when the door opened. "Kelly, how are you?" she asked in a voice that sounded like she'd been crying. "Sorry, but I don't have anything to report. Nothing more has happened since we last talked." As she spoke she tried to hide her face from Kelly.

Kelly could see why the lights in the room were dimmed and why Sandy was trying to avoid looking directly at her. There were two large bruises on Sandy's cheek and the skin around her left eye was black and blue. Even though it was a warm day, she had a sweater on over a blouse which was buttoned up to her neck.

"Sandy, I'm not here about the dog tag," she said in a soft voice. "When I was here yesterday, you moved into the sunlight, and I noticed a large bruise on your cheek, and it looked to me like you'd tried to cover it up with pancake makeup. Today I can see several new bruises, and those are only the ones I can see. The clothes you're wearing could be covering more. As you know, my husband's the Beaver County Sheriff, and he's had to deal with a number of spousal abuse cases. Over the course of our conversations about it, I've learned what to look for when a spouse is being abused. Your bruises look like classic cases of spousal abuse. Please, let me help you," Kelly said as she reached out and put her hand on Sandy's shoulder in a comforting gesture.

"Kelly, please, I beg of you to just forget what you saw. If Hank knew you suspected anything, he'd kill me."

"I sincerely hope that's an exaggeration. I think I need to call my husband. Spousal abuse is a felony in this state."

Kelly saw the terror in Sandy's eyes. "No, no, please don't call him. Hank promised me when he left this morning it would never happen again. He's going to get some help when he gets back from his business trip. I know he loves me. Sometimes he just can't help himself. He was crying when he left. After it happens, he's always so sorry about it. He doesn't mean to hurt me. It's like there's another person in him that comes out. Anyway, it was all my fault. I asked for it."

"What do you mean you asked for it?"

"I noticed how you looked at me yesterday, and I was pretty sure you could see the bruise. I figured since you were married to a sheriff you'd know what the bruise was from. I told Hank about it last night when we went out to dinner."

"What did he say?"

"He said it was my fault for not putting on enough makeup. On the way home from dinner he got angrier and angrier about it. I apologized and told him it would never happen again. When we got home he yelled at me that he'd make sure it didn't. He punched and kicked me so many times I finally collapsed and fell on the floor. I kept telling him the baby could get hurt if he didn't stop."

"The baby? What are you talking about? Oh no, Sandy, are you pregnant?"

"Yes. I'm two months along, and I was worried something would happen to the baby. That's when Hank stopped hitting me. He told me he was glad Mary was dead, so she couldn't poison my mind with all the bad things she was telling me about Hank."

"Sandy, I have no idea what you're talking about."

"One time I told Hank that even though Mary never said anything, I was pretty sure she'd noticed my bruises. When I told her I was pregnant, she sat me down and told me Hank needed to get some help, and that I should get some counselling too. When I told him what Mary had said he was furious."

"How long ago was that?"

"Probably about a week or so. I just found out two weeks ago I was pregnant, and I told Mary because I knew she'd have to get a replacement for me at Doggie Love."

"Sandy, let me help you. A good friend of mine is a psychologist. Her name is Liz, and she's married to a doctor who's also a good friend of mine. They're both very discreet, and no one will ever know about this. I'm sure they can also help your husband. When do you expect him to return from his business trip?"

"He's coming home tomorrow evening," she said, trying to keep the tears that had welled up in her eyes from flowing down her cheeks. "I want to talk to him first before I see anyone. He promised it would never happen again, and I know how much he wants our baby."

"Sandy, I hate to say this, but from what my husband has told me, every man who's involved in a spousal abuse case says the same thing. You can't put your baby's life at risk."

"Kelly, I'm sure Hank means it this time. I'm going to give him another chance. You can't make either one of us see a psychologist."

"That's true, but you might tell your husband if it ever happens again I'll make sure he's arrested for spousal abuse and prosecuted to the full extent of the law."

"You don't know him. He's a wonderful man. Anyway, I have to go. It's late, and I need to eat something. You know how fragile we newly pregnant women are."

"Yes, Sandy, I'm well aware how very fragile you are right now. Take care of yourself. I want to give you my cell phone number and the number at the coffee shop. If you feel you need to talk to someone, please call me."

"Thanks, I will. Now go on, I have to turn off my computer and lock up."

As Kelly walked back to her minivan, she felt sick thinking about the conversation that had just taken place. *I know it's going to happen again. His anger is classic and so is her response to it. I just hope the baby will be all right. The little innocent had no part in this. Life sometimes isn't fair, particularly to those who have no voice, such as unborn children and animals.*

CHAPTER TWENTY-FIVE

When she got home Kelly pulled her minivan into the driveway next to Mike's county sheriff's car. She pressed the garage door opener and drove into the garage. Although she didn't think Skyy would run away, she didn't want to take any chances, so she closed the garage door before opening the minivan's rear door for the dogs.

"In you go, kids. Mike's already home and that means Lady is too. I'll get your dinner in a minute." She walked into the house as the two dogs scampered in front of her. "Mike, we're home. Sorry we're late. Hope you didn't worry."

"Are you kidding?" he said, coming out of the kitchen. "I always worry when you're not where you're supposed to be, but I felt better knowing you had Rebel with you. Thought you might be able to use this," he said, handing her a glass of wine.

"You're right about that. The last couple of hours have been very challenging. Let me get the dogs fed, and then I'll tell you all about it, but first this little one needs to go outside." She opened the patio door for Skyy who was whimpering in front of the door.

A few minutes later she said, "Mike, if you believe in miracles, I think one just took place. Skyy whimpered and then ran outside when I opened the door. I can see that she's communing with nature at this very moment. This is definitely a good omen for the young pup."

"Couldn't agree more. Now if we can just teach her to stop running around the house with a roll of toilet paper in her mouth or from chewing on our glasses, she might just get my vote to stay."

"I'll see what I can do," Kelly said grinning. "But right now I really need to talk to you. I'm troubled by some things I learned today."

"Yeah, I can hear it in your voice. Let's go sit down in the great room, and we can talk." After they sat down on the large couch that faced the windows which looked out onto the bay Mike turned to her and said, "What's wrong?"

She told him she'd talked to someone earlier in the day who mentioned that Hank Reston had a very bad temper, or as the person had said, he had anger issues. Then she went on to tell Mike about her visit to the kennel and her conversation with Sandy.

"What do you think?" she asked.

"Exactly what you're thinking. It sounds like a classic case of spousal abuse, but I'm not sure how it fits into Mary's murder."

"Just listen to me for a minute. I need to talk this out and see if I can make something fit. I've had a lot of thoughts floating around in my head since my conversation with her. What if Hank got really angry when Sandy told him Mary had said they needed to seek counselling concerning his anger issues because she was pregnant? Maybe he wasn't planning on murdering Mary, but instead he wanted to damage her reputation with her customers by letting the dogs loose. Let's say Mary saw him do it and confronted him. He saw red, became violent, and killed her. That's one scenario that might work."

"Kelly, from what you're telling me that's entirely possible, but how can anyone prove it?"

"Maybe Sandy knows and isn't saying anything because she doesn't want her husband to go to prison. Maybe you could arrest him for spousal abuse and see if he'll admit to anything else once you start questioning him down at the jail."

"Sounds good on paper, Kelly, but it doesn't work that way. First of all, if a wife is unwilling to accuse her husband of spousal abuse and no one else can attest to it happening, he can't be arrested. That's the major problem with cases like that. Typically, the wife lives in fear of her husband and won't cooperate by testifying against him. That's the first thing that presents a problem."

"And the second one?"

"Pretty much the same scenario. Even if Sandy knows her husband killed Mary, without her testimony and no witnesses, my hands and the court's hands are tied."

"So what you're telling me is we wait around to see if he kills Sandy or the baby, and if someone sees him do it, then he can be charged with murder. Hate to say it Sheriff, but that sucks. Two lives are possibly being placed in danger and there's nothing you can do about it? Is that what I'm hearing you say?"

"Pretty much, and believe me, I don't like it any better than you do, but the law is very clear. My hands are completely tied at this point; however, I will say that he's now number one on my list of suspects."

"Fat lot of good that will do. So far we're talking about one murder. Wait until there's another one. There's got to be something more that can be done."

"The only thing that can be done is for Sandy to be willing to testify against him. She needs to be convinced that it would be best for everyone if she'd point her finger at him."

"Mike, I know you have ways that you can get her home address. Would you see if you can do that while I fix dinner? Maybe if I paid her a visit at her home I'd have better luck, particularly since her husband won't be back until tomorrow evening."

"I'm not sure I want you to go to her home. I don't feel very comfortable about you doing that. It could turn out to be a dangerous confrontational scene."

"I'll take Rebel with me. Sandy isn't a threat and since Hank's gone, there's nothing to worry about."

"Kelly, if I've learned one thing about you, it's that there's always something to worry about when you want to go off on your own while trying to catch a killer. I'll see what I can do," Mike said in a resigned voice as he walked down the hall to his home office.

CHAPTER TWENTY-SIX

At nine the next morning Kelly had just returned from walking Skyy in a grassy area near the pier when Roxie said, "There's a call on the telephone for you. I told the woman you'd be with her in a minute." Kelly put Skyy back in the storeroom and secured the latch on the gate. She walked over to the telephone extension and said, "This is Kelly Reynolds. May I help you?"

"Oh, I'm so glad you took my call. It's Sandy Reston. I really need to talk to you. Could you come out to my house? Please? If you don't, I think I'll lose my nerve."

"Of course. I believe you told me you were in one of the new developments south of town. What's the address?" She didn't want Sandy to know that Mike had found the address the evening before and given it to her. She listened carefully, and then said, "It will take me about twenty minutes. Are you all right?"

"I'm fine. I've made some important decisions about Hank and our relationship, and I really need to talk to you."

"See you in a few minutes." Kelly took off her apron and walked into the front area of the coffee shop. "Roxie, I need to leave for a little while. I'm going to take Rebel with me, but would you walk Skyy in about an hour if I'm not back by then?"

"Love to. That little girl is getting to me. She's adorable. I think I'll call her wiggle butt. She shakes her rear end so hard when she's wagging her tail, it looks like she's made of two parts," she said laughing. "Go on, we'll be fine."

"Come on, Rebel. I want you with me." They got in the minivan and drove south of Cedar Bay to where Sandy Renton lived. Kelly easily found her house and parked her minivan in front of it. "You stay here, Rebel. I shouldn't be too long. Probably better tell Mike where I am."

She took her phone out of her purse as she opened the door of the minivan. She pressed in Mike's number and heard his answerphone message, "You've reached Sheriff Reynolds. I'm not available to take your call at the moment. If this is an emergency, please call 911, otherwise I'll return your call as soon as possible." She decided there was no need to leave a message with Mike as it would probably just cause him to worry about her.

She put the phone in the pocket of her jeans and walked towards the house. Just as she sensed that someone was behind her she heard a voice say, "What you feel in your back is a gun. I have no problem with having to pull the trigger, but I would prefer it if we both went inside where Sandy is, and we can talk. After all, it's her fault you've even here."

Hank pushed open the door of the two story tract house. Kelly saw Sandy sitting on the sofa crying. "I am so sorry, Kelly. You've never met him, but this is my husband, Hank. He came home early from his business trip and wanted to know what I'd done during the day. I made the mistake of telling him about our conversation." There were fresh black and blue marks on her upper arms and a small gash on her forehead.

"Sit down, Kelly," Hank said. "You and I are going to take a little ride out of town in a few minutes. Don't want anything to go down here at the house. The neighbors might hear something and call your husband. That would be rich, wouldn't it? He comes to the house for a disturbing the peace call and finds his wife dead," Hank said laughing. "No, I have something much better planned. There's a small abandoned shack out on my employer's lumber property that no one knows about. I discovered it by accident one day a few months ago. Make a nice place to meet your maker. Sandy, say goodbye to Kelly."

"Kelly, It's all my fault. Hank told me he'd hurt the baby if I didn't call you. I can't hurt my baby," she said, sobbing.

Hank said in a smooth comforting voice, "Don't worry, Sandy, I'll be back in a little while and everything will be okay. Trust me. Our baby will be fine. Now that Mary's gone, and Kelly will soon be gone, there won't be any reason for me to get angry anymore. You know how much I love you. I'm doing this for you and our baby," Hank said, gently wiping Sandy's tears away.

He turned to Kelly. "I want you to walk over to the door that leads to the garage. I'll have my gun on you the whole time so don't even think about trying to make a run for it. I'm going to tie your hands behind you with some rope. When I'm through doing that I want you to get into the back seat of the silver car in the garage and lie down. If I sense you're trying anything, I'll shoot you. Do you understand?"

"Yes," she stammered, doing exactly what he asked. A few moments later he put the car in reverse, backed out of the driveway, and began driving. "This will take a few minutes. Just stay where you are and don't get up until I tell you to." He turned on the radio to a music station and hummed along with the singer.

Kelly felt the car make a series of turns. She snuck a peek and saw that they were in a heavily forested area. She didn't know who he worked for or where they were, but she sensed that her life was about to end.

Why didn't I take Rebel into the house with me? Really stupid of me. Mike has no idea where I am, nor does anyone else. It's just me and Hank Reston. This is not how I wanted my life to end. Alone in the forest with a crazy man who has a gun. I guess the only thing I can do is maybe buy a little time, and see if I can get him to talk to me.

"Hank, what are you going to name your child?"

"We're still talking about it. We haven't found out yet whether it's a boy or a girl. We'll get serious about the name once we know that."

"I'm curious about something. It's pretty apparent you were the one who killed Mary Barnes, but I don't understand why. Since it looks like I'm not going to ever be able to tell anyone, I really would like to know."

"I didn't plan on killing Mary. I let the dogs out to teach her a lesson, not to snoop in other people's lives. She told Sandy we should see a shrink because of a couple of small black and blue marks Sandy had on her face. Course she deserved them, but I guess Mary didn't see it that way. Anyway, I'd just let the last of the dogs out when Mary came out of the office and saw me. I didn't know she was in there. I didn't have a choice, so I hit her over the head with an iron bar that was lying on the ground next to the kennel. I didn't think about it, I just acted on instinct. I was wearing rubber latex gloves, so I wasn't worried about them finding my fingerprints on the iron bar. I had to keep my fingerprints off the kennel closures, because if fingerprints were found somebody would find out I had a couple of problems with the law a few years ago."

"I didn't think you could practice law if you had problems like that," Kelly said.

"You can't. The man who hired me at the lumber mill wanted my legal knowledge, but knew I couldn't practice in a court of law. Although my license was pulled because of those little problems, everybody's happy now. I got a job, and he gets legal advice for a lot less than he'd pay a lawyer licensed by the state. If they need an attorney, he has one he uses, and I act as an adviser. It's a win-win situation for everyone. That's enough talking. We're here. I'm going to open the car door and step back. I want you to walk over to the shack. Once we're inside, I'll use the silencer, and you'll be history. Nobody's around, so I'll have plenty of time to dig a grave and voila, no more Kelly Reynolds."

Kelly started to walk towards the shack, but then stopped and looked up, silently praying. *Please, please help me.*

"By the way, you can forget about asking anyone for help. Prayers aren't heard out here. Now quit stalling and get in the shack."

Knowing she was taking the last few steps of her life, Kelly walked through the door of the shack.

CHAPTER TWENTY-SEVEN

Mike had just returned to his office from a meeting he'd had with several of his deputies giving them an update on the Barnes murder case. Unfortunately, there wasn't much to tell them. There were plenty of suspects, but none of them had emerged as someone who could be arrested for the murder. When he sat down at his desk he glanced at his phone and saw that Kelly had called him but hadn't left a message, which was very unusual for her.

Several months earlier he'd read about the Messages app on the iPhones for texts which allowed a person to continuously keep track of where someone else was physically located. He and Kelly had agreed it would be a good thing to do, so they'd always know where the other one was, particularly if they were running late. Mike clicked on her name and hit location. He looked at his watch and was sure the location would show that she was at the coffee shop. It didn't. It showed she was south of Cedar Bay, actually quite a distance from the coffee shop. He kept hitting refresh, and he saw that she was moving in a southwesterly direction.

Something's wrong. This is not like her. I better see what's going on.

"Back later. Had something come up. If I have any appointments in the next couple of hours, cancel them. I'll call you when I know more," he said to his secretary as he ran out the door. "Take care of Lady for me." When he got in the car, he called the coffee shop.

"Roxie, it's Mike. Where's Kelly?"

"I have no idea. She left about twenty minutes ago and said she'd be back later. Why?"

"I'm concerned about her. She called me and didn't leave a message. We have an agreement that if the other one couldn't answer the phone for some reason, we'd leave a message. Was Rebel with her when she left?"

"Yes, she asked if I would walk Skyy if she was gone over an hour, but she said she was taking Rebel with her."

"Good. Do you have any idea why she would be south of town? That's what the Message location on her phone is showing."

"I have no idea. The only thing that even rings a bell with me is that a day or so ago we were talking about a guy who had come into the coffee shop asking about Kelly, and I didn't recognize him, nor did anyone else at the coffee shop. We thought that was kind of strange. I remember making a comment that there were several new developments south of town and maybe he lived there."

"Yes, and that's also where the manager of the Doggie Love Kennel and her husband live. I'm pretty sure that's who the man was. I'm heading down there now. If she calls or shows up, let me know immediately."

"Will do, and I'd appreciate if you would call me as soon as you know anything. I don't need to remind you about the kind of trouble Kelly can get into."

"No, you don't. Talk to you later," he said, aware of the pounding in his chest and his increased pulse rate. *I know it has something to do with the manager's husband. I don't know how or why, but in my gut I know. I just hope I get there in time.*

He sped up and switched on his siren and red lights. Mike radioed two of his deputies and told them to start heading south, and he'd let them know where to go specifically when he knew. He wasn't a particularly religious man, but he began to fervently pray. He remembered the saying from World War II about there being no atheists in foxholes and thought that probably applied to him when it came to Kelly's welfare.

Mike jammed his foot on the brakes when he saw Kelly's car parked in front of the Reston's two-story home. He threw his car door open, raced up the steps, and banged on the door. "It's Sheriff Reynolds, Mrs. Reston, open up." A moment later Sandy opened the door, crying. "Where's Kelly? I know she's not here. Did your husband take her somewhere?"

"Yes, I have no idea where. He said he was going to kill her. It's all my fault..."

Mike dashed back to his car before she could finish her sentence. He saw Rebel in Kelly's minivan, opened the door, and yelled for Rebel to follow him. He looked down at the tiny blue dot on his phone which represented Kelly and again prayed he would get to her in time. With his siren screaming and his red lights flashing he raced to close the distance between his location and the flashing blue dot on his phone.

Mike looked at the cell phone on the seat next to him and several times hit the refresh button while he was driving. Each time he saw that he was getting closer to Kelly's location. The last time he refreshed it the dot didn't move, and he realized he was very close to where Kelly must be. He'd been so intent on following the blue dot that he hadn't paid much attention to the fact he'd turned onto a dirt road that led into a thickly forested area.

He turned off the siren and the red lights as he continued driving deeper into the heavily wooded area. He stopped his car when he saw a silver car about twenty yards ahead of him. To the left of it, almost hidden from view, was a dilapidated old shack surrounded by trees. He radioed his deputies and gave them his coordinates and told them to hurry, and that they should turn off their red lights and siren when they turned onto the dirt road.

He quietly opened the car door, indicating for Rebel to follow him. The two of them silently made their way from tree to tree. He heard a voice coming from the shack. "If you were younger, I'd have you undress and have a little fun with you, but you're too old for my tastes. I want you to lie on the floor face down. I really don't want to see your face contort when I shoot you."

CHAPTER TWENTY-EIGHT

From his vantage point behind a tree Mike saw that the door of the shack was open. He quietly took his gun out of his holster. He could vaguely make out a man's form standing with his back to the open door, and what looked like a gun in the man's hand. Later, when Mike looked back on what happened in the next few moments, he realized there was no thought process involved in what he did. He'd acted purely from instinct.

"Drop the gun," Mike yelled, while at the same time shooting at the gun in the man's hand. Mike hadn't even needed to yell the words. His gunshot hit the man's hand, knocking the gun out of his hand and onto the floor. Rebel charged at Hank and attacked him, knocking him to the ground. He stood over him, snarling and snapping. "Rebel, stand guard." Mike picked up Hank's gun and hurried over to where Kelly was lying prone on the floor.

"Kelly, are you all right?" Mike asked, putting his hand on her shoulder. "It's okay, sweetheart. Turn over. I want to make sure you're okay." She rolled over and looked up at him.

"Oh, Mike, I thought this was going to be it. I was going to be murdered in a shack in a forest, and no one would ever find me. Hank said he was going to dig a grave and put me in it. How did you know where to look for me? Did Sandy tell you? I left Rebel in the car at her house, but I don't think she knew where Hank was going to take me. Mike, he's the one who killed Mary and let the dogs out."

She told him what Hank had told her about killing Mary, and Mike explained how he'd found her through the Message locater on his phone. A few moments later Mike heard voices and looked outside. His two deputies were hurrying up to the shack.

"I heard your voice, Sheriff, and figured you had everything under control. What do you want us to do?"

"First of all, handcuff this guy. His name is Hank Reston. Take him to the station. I want him arrested for the murder of Mary Barnes and the attempted murder of Kelly Reynolds. Kelly will be in tomorrow to give her statement."

"Boss, I can't get close enough to the guy to handcuff him because of the dog. Can you call him off?"

"Rebel, stand down. Good boy." Rebel backed away from Hank and walked over to Kelly, who was sitting on the floor. He put his big head on her shoulder, his way of asking for an ear scratch which she gladly gave him.

"Mike, my legs have turned to jelly. I'm not sure I can stand up, much less walk," she said starting to cry as the realization hit her that she was safe.

He bent down and helped her up. "Lean on my shoulder, sweetheart, and I'll get you to the car. You'll be okay in a few minutes. Rebel, come." He turned to his deputies. "Might want to wrap Reston's hand. Looks like I nicked him when I shot the gun out of his hand. I'll meet you at the station after I take Kelly home."

"Mike, I can't go home. I need to go back to the coffee shop. Roxie will never forgive me for leaving her with the lunch crowd."

"Not only will she forgive you, she'll be the first to insist that you take it easy the rest of the day. I'll pick up Skyy on the way home. Look at it this way, Roxie will have a great story to tell everyone. No one will mind if their lunch isn't served quite as fast as usual. Once Doc, your favorite lunchtime customer, finds out what's happened to you, he'll probably be knocking on the door at the house to make sure you're okay. No, there's only one place you're going and that's home."

"I can tell from the tone of your voice that I don't have much to say about this decision."

"You've got that right, sweetheart. I am personally making sure you're going to rest for the remainder of the day. I'll have a couple of my deputies get your minivan and take it to the house. Right now I need to call Roxie and let her know you're safe and sound. It's going to be kind of like one of those do you want the good news or the bad news things. The good news is that Kelly's okay. The bad news is she almost got murdered. Kelly, I'm beginning to think you're like a cat that has nine lives. Whatever it is, you've been very, very lucky."

"I know. I've thought the same thing about some of my past experiences, but today I was pretty sure my cat lives had come to an end. It never occurred to me you could find me. I am so thankful you did."

"So am I, and I have a confession to make."

"What is it?"

He looked away abashedly as he closed the passenger door of the car and walked around to the driver's side. After Mike got in the car he preoccupied himself with his seat belt and getting the car started. Finally, he spoke, "I kind of made a promise. It has to do with me deciding I'll be going to church with you this Sunday. It was kind of in exchange for me getting to you in time."

"That will make Father Brown very happy, and you know what? It makes me happy too, although I would prefer to have gotten you there a little less dramatically."

"Trust me, you're not the only one!"

CHAPTER TWENTY-NINE

It was after six when Mike and Lady walked through the front door that evening. "Kelly, I'm home. Where are you?" he called out.

"I'm in the great room looking out at the bay. No matter how many times I look at it, I'm still in awe that boats can float and maneuver their way on something so vast and not sink. I know all the engineers in the world cringe when I say that, but it's kind of like airplanes. I'll never figure out what makes them stay in the air. It's all quite amazing."

"And that's one of the reasons I love you. You still look at the world with childlike eyes and find wonder in it. How are you doing after the excitement of today?"

"I'm fine. At least Doc says I'm fine."

"So I was right? He did come here to examine you?"

"Yes. Roxie called and told me he left half his lunch uneaten he was in such a hurry to get here. That's quite a compliment, because that man loves his lunch. Anyway, he examined me, and said I was probably still somewhat in shock, but it would wear off pretty soon. Now that you've caught the bad guy, is anything else happening?"

"I went to the Reston's home and personally told Sandy I'd

arrested her husband for the murder of Mary Barnes. I asked if I could call anyone for her. She told me she had a sister who lived in Portland, and that she could probably come and stay with her for a few days. Even though Hank had told her he'd murdered Mary, she was still pretty shaken up when she realized that the father of her unborn child would likely be going to prison for a long time. She asked if you would call her tomorrow, so she could get the name and telephone number of the psychologist you'd recommended."

"I feel really sorry for her, but I'm so happy it sounds like she's going to address the spousal abuse issues. Of course Hank won't be able to participate in spousal abuse for a long time, but if she felt she deserved to be hit, it seems like she needs some counseling. Can she file a complaint against him for spousal abuse now that he's been arrested for murder?"

"She could, but what would be the point? It might add a little time to his sentence, but not much, and she probably needs to conserve her strength for her pregnancy. Murder and attempted murder is enough to put him away for a long, long time. He'll probably have great-grandchildren by the time he ever gets out of prison."

"I was thinking about what Ricky Anderson said about her – that things weren't always what they appeared to be. I wonder if he noticed the bruises, and that's why he said it."

"I don't know. I talked to Noelle, Mary's daughter, and told her that her mother's killer had been arrested. She was relieved that the criminal investigation part of her mother's death was out of the way. She told me she and her husband had made a decision to sell the property to a developer who had offered to buy it. He tried to buy the adjacent property that belongs to Susan Yates, but she wouldn't sell it to him. He told Noelle they were going to build a block wall fence so future owners wouldn't have to look at her run-down house and property."

"Did Noelle have anything else to say?"

"Yes. She asked how we were doing with Skyy. I told her Skyy was adapting to our family very well, other than a few incidences involving eyeglasses and toilet paper. Noelle said she hoped we'd keep her. I told her we were definitely not giving her up. Matter of fact, I've gotten to like that little bundle of fur. Speaking of which, where is she?"

"Oh, Mike. Other than you arriving at the shack just in the nick of time, that's the best news I've had all day, however, I haven't seen her for a while, and that makes me nervous."

"Stay where you are," Mike said, "I'll see if I can find her." He came back a moment later and motioned for Kelly to follow him. He put his finger to his lips, cautioning her not to say anything. She followed him down the hall to their bedroom and there on the floor was Rebel, sound asleep, with Skyy, at about one-quarter of his size, curled up next to him. Rebel sensed they were there, lazily opened one eye, and then closed it as if he was winking at them.

When they got back to the great room, Mike put his arms around Kelly and whispered in her ear, "It's all good, Kelly. It's all good."

RECIPES

BRIE AND EGG STRATA

Ingredients

2 tsp. olive oil
2 cups chopped onion
1 large Yukon gold potato, diced
1 cup chopped red bell pepper
1 cup halved grape tomatoes
1 tsp. salt, divided in half
¼ lb. ciabatta bread, cut in 1 inch cubes and toasted (You may also use a French baguette or sourdough bread)
Cooking spray
4 oz. Brie cheese, rind removed and chopped
1 cup egg substitute (usually comes in a cardboard container like cream)
2 large eggs
1 tsp. dried Herbes de Provence or an Italian herb mixture
¼ tsp. freshly ground pepper
3 cups milk
2 tbsp. chopped fresh parsley

Directions

Note: The beauty of this recipe is that you can prepare it the night before. If you're going to do that, combine the ingredients as directed below but without the egg mixture, then cover that mixture with plastic wrap and refrigerate. Combine the ingredients for the egg mixture and refrigerate in a separate container. Thirty minutes before you're ready to bake it pour the egg mixture over the bread mixture, and let it stand at room temperature.

Preheat the oven to 350 degrees and lightly spray a 9 x 13-inch glass dish. Heat the oil in a large nonstick skillet over medium-high heat. Add the onion, potato, and red bell pepper. Sauté about 4 minutes or until tender. Stir in ½ teaspoon salt. Combine onion mixture and bread.

Place half of the bread, onion, potato, and pepper mixture in the prepared baking dish and sprinkle with half of the Brie. Top with the remaining bread mixture and the remaining Brie.

Put the egg substitute and the eggs in a medium size bowl. Add the remaining ½ teaspoon salt, herbs de Provence, and pepper. Add the milk, whisking until well blended. Pour egg mixture over bread mixture and let stand for 30 minutes.

Bake at 350 degrees for 50 minutes or until set. Sprinkle with parsley and serve. Enjoy!

CORNISH GAME HENS WITH APRICOT STUFFING & ORANGE SAUCE

Ingredients for Stuffing Hens

4 Cornish game hens
1 cup orange juice
½ cup apricot brandy or regular brandy
8 oz. package cornbread stuffing mix
¾ cup chopped dried apricots (I use scissors to chop them. It seems to work well)
¼ cup butter

Directions

Preheat oven to 350 degrees. Heat the orange juice in a medium size saucepan. Add the brandy and butter and stir until the butter is melted. Add the apricots and simmer 2-3 minutes until they're tender. Add the stuffing mix and stir to blend. Remove from heat and use mixture to stuff game hens. (I know it's messy, but whenever I'm stuffing something like a turkey, I use my hands. Naturally, you're going to want to wash your hands before you ever start cooking!) Bake about 1 hour uncovered or until the hens are browned. Baste the hens when you first put them in the oven and again after 30 minutes.

Ingredients for Basting:
½ cup orange juice
2 tbsp. soy sauce

Directions:
Combine and set aside.

Ingredients for Orange Sauce:

2/3 cup brown sugar
2/3 cup granulated white sugar
3 tbsp. cornstarch
2 tbsp. grated orange peel
1 ½ cups orange juice
1/8 tsp. salt
½ cup apricot brandy or orange flavored liqueur

Directions:

Combine the sugars in a saucepan over medium heat. Add the cornstarch, orange peel, orange juice, salt, and liqueur. Stir while simmering until slightly thickened. Spoon the warm sauce over the game hens after they're removed from the oven and serve. Put the remaining sauce in a dish on the table. Enjoy!

EASY PEASY BAKED BEANS

Ingredients

1 can M & M baked beans
½ cup brown sugar
2 tbsp. chopped onions, lightly sautéed
½ cup catsup

Directions

Put all of the ingredients in a saucepan over medium heat. Stir to combine and when warm, serve. Enjoy!

KILLER DOUBLE/DOUBLE CHEESEBURGERS (MAKES TWO)

Sauce Ingredients

¼ cup catsup
½ cup mayonnaise
1 tsp yellow mustard (use the prepared, not the powder)
2 ¼ tsp. sweet pickle relish
2 ¼ tsp. dill pickle relish
1 tsp. Worcestershire sauce
1 tsp. white wine vinegar
½ tsp. salt
¼ tsp. sugar

Directions

Stir the ingredients together in a medium bowl and set aside. Sauce can be kept refrigerated up to two weeks. (I use it on all kinds of sandwiches.)

Cheeseburgers and Topping Ingredients:

½ lb. ground beef (try to get as close to 80/20 ratio as possible. I sometimes have to mix two different packages of ground beef together to get the right ratio)
8 iceberg lettuce leaves
4 large tomato slices
½ yellow onion, thinly sliced (separate them into rings)
4 slices American or Swiss cheese
4 soft white hamburger buns (I use the cheap plain ones - no sesame seeds, onion, etc.)
¼ tsp. salt

Directions:

Heat a griddle or a heavy skillet over medium heat until very hot. Measure out 4 two ounce patties and flatten to about ¼ inch thick. Toast the cut sides of the buns on the griddle. Cook the burgers on one side for about 45 seconds. Flip them and put a slice of cheese on each one, frying them for an additional 45 seconds. Remove from the heat.

Assembly:

Put a tablespoon of sauce on the bottom and top sections of the bun. On the bottom of each bun, put two lettuce leaves, a cheeseburger, a slice of tomato, onion rings, and then the second burger. Enjoy!

FISHERMAN'S FRIED RICE

Ingredients

1 cup white rice
2 cups water
8 strips bacon
8 green onions, chopped

8 eggs, whisked in small bowl
3 tbs. soy sauce
4 pats of butter
Salt and pepper to taste

Directions

Place the rice and water in a medium saucepan and bring to a boil. Reduce the heat to a simmer and cover for 20 minutes. After 20 minutes remove the cover and continue to cook 6-8 minutes to reduce moisture content in rice.

Fry the bacon in a 12-inch frying pan until crisp. Remove, drain on a paper towel, cool, and crumble. Put the crumbled bacon in a small dish and set aside. Drain half of the bacon grease into a separate bowl, add the cooked rice to frying pan and fry the rice on medium high heat for 10-12 minutes, stirring occasionally so that the rice gets evenly browned.

Add additional bacon grease as needed. Add chopped onions and bacon pieces and gently combine into rice. With a spatula, push the rice mixture to one side of the frying pan, add the butter to the empty side of the pan. Once the butter is melted pour in the egg mixture and cook on medium heat, as if making soft scrambled eggs.

When the eggs are slightly firm, flip them and using the edge of the spatula cut the cooked eggs into small bite size strips 1-2 inches long and ½ inch wide. Combine the rice mixture with the cooked egg strips and add soy sauce, stirring gently. Add salt and pepper to taste. Spoon equal portions of cooked mixture onto serving plates and place soy sauce on the table. Serves four. Enjoy early in the morning before the sun comes up and then go fishing!

Amazing Ebooks & Paperbacks for FREE

Go to www.dianneharman.com/freepaperback.html and get your FREE copies of Dianne's books and Dianne's favorite recipes immediately by signing up for her newsletter.

Once you've signed up for her newsletter you're eligible to win autographed paperbacks. One lucky winner is picked every week. Hurry before the offer ends.

ABOUT THE AUTHOR

Dianne lives in Huntington Beach, California, with her husband, Tom, a former California State Senator, and her boxer dog, Kelly. Her passions are cooking, reading, and dogs, so whenever she has a little free time, you can either find her in the kitchen, playing with Kelly in the back yard, or curled up with the latest book she's reading.

Her award winning books include:

Cedar Bay Cozy Mystery Series
Kelly's Koffee Shop, Murder at Jade Cove, White Cloud Retreat, Marriage and Murder, Murder in the Pearl District, Murder in Calico Gold, Murder at the Cooking School, Murder in Cuba, Trouble at the Kennel

Liz Lucas Cozy Mystery Series
Murder in Cottage #6, Murder & Brandy Boy, The Death Card, Murder at The Bed & Breakfast, The Blue Butterfly

High Desert Cozy Mystery Series
Murder & The Monkey Band, Murder & The Secret Cave

Coyote Series
Blue Coyote Motel, Coyote in Provence, Cornered Coyote

Website: www.dianneharman.com
Blog: www.dianneharman.com/blog
Email: dianne@dianneharman.com

Newsletter
If you would like to be notified of her latest releases please go to www.dianneharman.com and sign up for her newsletter.